GUNPLAY AT SWEETWATER SPRINGS

By the same author

Black Widow

Gunplay at Sweetwater Springs

NEWTON KETTON

A Black Horse Western

ROBERT HALE · LONDON

First published in Great Britain 1996

ISBN 0 7090 5776 8

Robert Hale Limited
Clerkenwell House
Clerkenwell Green
London EC1R 0HT

Photoset in North Wales by
Derek Doyle & Associates, Mold, Clwyd.
Printed in Great Britain by
St Edmundsbury Press Ltd, Bury St Edmunds, Suffolk.
Bound by WBC Book Manufacturers Limited,
Bridgend, Mid-Glamorgan.

For all those connected
with
Newton Ketton
with love and affection.

ONE

I had to thank Amelia for turning me from a boy into a man. She did it the hard way and I never forgave her for it. I was a twenty-year-old and not used to females, my own ma dying when I was six, and I was brought up rough by my pa and Uncle Jed.

Life was hard on the ranch. I knew more about cows than I did about womenfolk, so when this Quaker family came riding by looking for land to settle on, I fell hook, line and sinker for the demure little blonde who kept her blue eyes safely on the ground.

They were a psalm-singing lot and because they rode twenty miles every Sunday morning to Sweetwater Springs to the little wooden church, I followed suit and got me a bit of religion that I otherwise wouldn't have got.

Pa was against all this fooling about. I did my

Sunday-morning chores on Saturday night to make up the time, but he wasn't satisfied. It took time and effort to woo Miss Amelia Hitchens and the harder it was, the keener I was to become leg-shackled. I kept my brains in my breeches in those days and couldn't wait to kiss her.

The upshot was, that that first kiss got her all a-screaming and a-crying and her sanctimonious pa had us married before I knew what was what, despite my pa and Uncle Jed going rampaging to their home to protest.

It turned out that Amelia was older than I thought, and frigid, not that I had any idea at the time. I thought all women just lay back and did their duty and then went back to butter-making and stitching and the hundred and one jobs women liked to do.

One thing I learned, and that was to wash regular. She would soon wrinkle her nose up if I came to bed smelling of horses or cows, and pig muck she couldn't abide.

She was sweet and clean herself, and was forever washing clothes and using the smoothing iron. My pa got sick of all the women's gear hanging about, and us all getting entangled in white linen shifts and bloomers. He wasn't a man for changing his ways and he liked his liquor and he liked women too.

It was a pity he hadn't told me about all those

fancy women in Sweetwater Springs. I might not have been in such a hurry to get hog-tied to Amelia.

But the mistake was made and for ten years we lived a life of compromise. We had three children, Billy, Tommy and Tabitha and I can safely say that the only time I enjoyed her body was when those children were conceived, for the truth of it was, that as soon as she knew she was in the family way, she up and took to sleeping in the children's room and I had to settle for nights alone.

I soon found that the blue eyes were cold and hard. She resented the fact we shared a small cabin with Pa and Uncle Jed. She wanted her own home which was impossible. We hadn't the cash for a new barn never mind another house.

The only time I saw her smile was when we went to Sweetwater Springs on Sunday and she could parade her children to the townsfolk. But all that stopped the Sunday morning that Alice Symons came to church and waved to me and whispered in a hoarse tone that everyone could hear that she would see me on the next Saturday night.

She made it clear what we'd both be up to. I could have throttled her. I saw Amelia's thin mouth close like a trap. By all this, it can be seen that I wasn't the naive young boy any more and what I wasn't getting at home I was getting elsewhere and to hell with it!

The outcome was that Amelia stopped going to church and so did I. I think the kids suffered, but they were little and there would be time for all that when they were older.

But Amelia made life hell. I never realized the depths to which a vindictive woman could sink, to get her revenge. It came to me that Amelia just didn't like men, any men, not only me her husband, I asked her why she had taken a shine to me and married me if she felt as she did. Her answer was that she wanted to fulfil her role in life and have children but she didn't need a man in the carnal sense. She only needed a man to give her shelter and protection.

Big deal!

I never forgave her for that and it bit real deep. When she died aged thirty-five from blood-poisoning from a horse-fly, I buried her beside my ma in the little plot we had fenced off, and I didn't shed a tear. It was a relief.

But there were problems. Pa and Uncle Jed weren't as spry as they used to be and Billy was only nine and Tommy going on eight and Tabby young enough to need a woman to look after her.

So I went to town to look for a suitable housekeeper. That was when I rode into other problems. Respectable women wouldn't hear tell of coming to an all-male establishment and the fancy women didn't want to look after three children ... they could make more money on their backs than I could afford to pay.

So the kids grew independent and wild. They had no manners, no education and no discipline, for I hadn't the least idea how to handle them and Pa and Uncle Jed doted on them and as far as they were concerned, couldn't do no wrong.

The crunch came one day when their grandparents, the Hitchens's, came for their half-yearly visit. They expected the kids to be lined up waiting to receive them, all spit and polish. Of course the little devils went missing. They'd gone to play down by the nearly dry creek and for some reason the boys started a humdinger, pasting hell out of each other. Tabby interfered, as she usually did, and the boys turned on her and blackened her eye and cut her lip as a lesson to let them get on with things that were none of her business.

She took it in good part but the grandparents didn't. They wanted to take her right back to their piddling little dirt farm down the valley and turn her into another ladylike Amelia.

Neither she nor I were having any of that. She kicked and screamed when the old man took a grip of her. I drew my gun and believe me, if he hadn't been Tabby's kin, I'd have put a bullet in him. Inside, I was as mean as I looked on the outside.

That was the day the feuding began.

That was the day when the townsfolk of Sweetwater Springs turned against all the Drexel family and the riders of the DXL ranch.

Old Hitchens made his mouth go amongst his God-fearing friends, but of course what he told them was exaggerated a hundred-fold. Folk in town always find time to gossip and they were no better in the saloons than they were in the Ladies' Sewing Bee, so that the first time we rode in shutters went up, and we could get no supplies or services.

Not that I minded. We could always get dry goods from Wichita but I felt the insult when the local whorehouse locked its doors against us. That was coming it a bit too far, considering who they were ....

As for the saloons, we didn't give a toss. Old Pete Bean had the scruffiest joint in town but he'd been a pal of Pa's for years and his doors were still open to us.

'I never did hold with those psalm-singing bastards,' he muttered, 'and I still owe your pa for what he did for me way back in 'sixty-five.'

'Yeh, we know,' I said hastily. I'd heard the story about Pa saving him at the end of the war ever since I as knee-high to a rattlesnake. 'Just set 'em up all round while we think what to do about this here town.'

He leant forward and whispered in my ear. 'If I was you, I'd wait until nightfall and blow up the stores and go in and rape all the bloody women, like we did during the war!'

I laughed. 'We're not at war, Pete. We'll have to do something less drastic.'

But by the time me and the boyos had got a skinful we still hadn't come to any conclusions about what we should do. So we went back to the ranch to ponder over it.

But I soon found out where Amelia had got her vengeful spirit. That old man, good Quaker as he was, was poison. It got beyond a joke and when Jesse Coates was found dead in supsicious circumstances, the rumour went round that it was to do with the DXL ranch.

Trouble, was, Jesse was a bit of a troublemaker. His place abutted ours and there'd always been disputes on his side about water rights. Pa and Uncle Jed had always been easy-oasy about letting him water his cattle on our land. But when the drought struck three years running, we had to kind of ration his stock. He didn't like that and when the whispering campaign started, he added his own fuel to the fire.

The first I knew about it was when Tommy came home from riding fence on a lathered horse, his face grey with dust. I ran out of the barn and Pa managed to hobble down from the veranda to see what was up. We could see Tommy was about all in, for as a fourteen year-old he couldn't match Billy for muscles or strength. He's the bookish type is Tommy, more brains than brawn.

'What's happened? Has there been an accident?'

I'd sent them out both together to ride the fence. I thought it would keep 'em both out mischief but now my heart clenched on itself. 'Tommy, what is it?'

He was lying on the ground, gasping for breath and Pa was holding him.

'It's Billy, Pa. They come and dragged him away ....' Tommy was choking and gagging for breath. Beside us stood the little mustang that Tommy favoured, and she was quivering as if her legs would give way. I knew he'd ridden far and fast.

'Who's they, Tommy? Come on, boy, answer me!' I pulled him roughly out of Pa's arms and shook him. His eyes widened in shock. I think he always knew that Billy was my favourite.

'Careful, Hal, the boy's about to collapse,' Pa growled at me and I was hit with remorse and I hugged him to me. 'Come on, Tommy, spit it all out and we can go get Billy.'

Tommy struggled away from me and managed to sit up. I was conscious somewhere in the back of my mind of Tommy's withdrawal from me but I would deal with it later. For me, it was Billy who was most important ... a decision that was going to mean much heartache later on.

Tommy's eyes flickered and then helpless tears overflowed.

'It was a posse from the town ... we was helpless. We was at Twobit Creek digging out the water-hole near that bit of old fencing when they came ....'

'And?' I was conscious of a burning hate streaking through me like fire. Tommy swallowed and summoned up more strength.

'We was like two newborn calves, knowing nothing and expecting nothing. We thought they'd come to ask directions. Instead ....' He gulped and shook his head disbelievingly. 'Tad Grainger took out his gun and shot between Billy's feet and before either of us could get over the shock, they were on us like flies on blood.' He turned to me, a hopeless pleading in his eyes. 'We fought 'em, Pa. We fought 'em good but there were too many.'

'But why? Why take Billy to town?'

My pa answered that one.

'It's clear, ain't it? They're wanting a fallguy for that murder. Was old man Hitchens with them, boy?'

Tommy shook his head.

'No, but Ned Hitchens and his brother Bob were there and a whole parcel of Godfearing lickarses from the church!'

I felt myself stiffen at the mention of the

church. If I had my way. I'd burn it down and build another. For me, the present one was desecrated by the hypocrites that ran it. The very name Hitchens made my blood run hot and cold all at the same time.

'Right, bring in the boys, Pa. Rattle the dinner bell good because we're riding into town.'

'I'm coming with you, Pa.' Tommy looked resolute but white and his eyes looked black in his thin face.

'No, you're to stay home and be on hand for your grandpa and Uncle Jed. Besides you're too young ....' I turned away from him but not before I saw his look. I turned back to him and put a hand on his shoulder. 'Son, you did good and I'm proud of you but you're only fourteen. I don't want to make a man of you yet!'

'Why not, Pa? I'm doing a man's work on the ranch, and have done so ever since I could walk!'

'Yes, well, work never killed anyone but when it comes to fighting ....' I stopped to make certain of what I really meant. Then I said slowly, 'Work is one thing but when it comes to gunplay nothing takes away a boy's youth quicker than a killing. I don't want you tasting that kind of blood yet, Tommy. It tends to become a habit and a young feller with the bloodlust doesn't last long. There's always someone faster. The whole of the West is littered with graves of cocky young roosters trying to make names for themselves. I don't want to set you on that path, Tommy.'

'But Pa, it's our Billy in that town jail! I've got a right ....'

'No, you haven't, boy. I'm his pa and I've got the right. Now you do as I say. The oldsters need looking after and if I know you're with them, I'll not worry.' I smiled at him but he wasn't really convinced. I knew, or I thought I did, what was in his mind. It was his own brother in the town jail and he and Billy were very close.

I didn't wait to see if my words had the right effect. I went off to check my rifle and load up with shells. If those townsfolk wouldn't listen to reason then we'd take Billy by force and to hell with 'em!

There was to be no time for reasoning. When me and the boys rode into town there was an unholy scattering of men from in front of the jail.

The door was being battered in and the sheriff and his deputy just about overpowered. We were just in time to stop a lynching.

We came thundering down the street, me and the boys, all hardened cases and ready for a fight. Guns exploded skywards and we caused mayhem with dogs and women howling and the men of the town diving for cover. They were not so brave when it came to facing hard-arsed cowboys, these soft townsfolk, as they were when they howled for the life of a frightened youngster.

We galloped our way through the mass and as Mickey O'Rourke fanned the crowd with his gun, I slid to the ground and forced my way into the jail where Sheriff Tomlin waited with his deputy.

'Thank God you're here, Drex,' he panted. 'It was getting a bit hairy. Another half-hour and they would have strung the lad up without a hearing. I couldn't hold them much longer.'

He wiped his sweating forehead on a dirty bandanna.

'Where is he?' I wasn't in the mood for small talk.

'In the farthest cell. Jesse Coates's foreman swears your Billy killed him and as he's sparking the preacher's daughter, all the churchmen are going along with it.'

'What about Hitchens?'

'He's kept out of it, but his nephews are in it up to their ears.'

'You know what this means, Sheriff?'

'Yeh, there's going to be gunplay in Sweetwater Springs!'

I lost no more time but went looking for Billy.

What they'd done to Billy made me more angry than I'd ever been in my life. The kid's face was bruised and black and I hardly recognized him. Silently the sheriff handed me the key to the cell.

'They brought him in like that, Drex. I had nothing to do with it.'

'I believe you, Sheriff.' I pulled my boy into my arms and held him close. We're not a demonstrative family but at that moment we were welded as one. I felt his hurt and fear and for once he was a little boy again wanting his pa's support.

Then I put him from me.

'Let's get back to the ranch.'

'Take him out the back way, Drex, and you'd better knock me out. I've to live with these people. No need to get on the wrong side of them.'

I didn't answer, but gave him a quick one on the jaw, not enough to damage him but enough to cause a bruise and look good.

Then I put an arm about Billy and I hustled him out of the back door.

Outside, a tall gangly woman was hanging out washing in the next yard to the jail. Vaguely I knew her for the sheriff's sister and she was the town's schoolmarm. Ruth Lowrie was a widow woman and a plain one at that. She paused in hanging up her brother's drawers.

'Bring him into the house. I'll put arnica on them there bruises.'

'Thank you, ma'am, but it's best we be on our way.'

'He's in no fit state to ride. Joe says his body is as black as his face.'

I faced her grimly.

'If he can't ride, I'll carry him.'

She nodded in acceptance. 'Very well, Mister Drexel, but if he takes bad come for me, for I don't think Doc Carruthers will come. He's an upholder of the church!'

'Thank you, ma'am. I'll remember that.' Without another look at her, I half carried, half hauled Billy away.

TWO

It was while I was hauling Billy home I thought of Tabby. She hadn't come running out of the cabin when Tommy had come storming in. That meant she hadn't been around the buildings anywhere at the time.

It was nothing new for that girl to go off on her own. At ten, she was an independent little cuss, a bit dreamy when she wasn't in one of her paddywoosters as Pa called them. I would have to do something about that girl and soon, for she reminded me of a young mare ready to be broken in. I didn't relish the job because although I could handle wayward horses, a wild undisciplined female was another pot of beans.

Now I had stirrings of fear. What if the silly wench had somehow got wind of what happened, and decided to poke her pretty nose into none of her business?

It was as I feared when we reached the ranch. Billy was safe home and now the other two were missing. I could have bit dust!

Pa was all apologetic.

'Never missed the young varmints until it was time to eat. Rang the bell but it was only me and Jed to eat the vittles. What d'you think got into their noddles, Hal?'

'I don't know, but I'll put a sting in their breeches when I get hold of them!'

Mickey O'Rourke, who acted as *segundo* when I was otherwise engaged, came to me looking serious.

'I've just been talking to the old prospector. He saw the two kids riding like the wind past his diggings. He hollered after them but they took no heed, but they were heading to the Hitchens's place.'

'Thanks Mickey. You and the boys come and get your grub, then get them back to work. I'm going to pay a visit to the Hitchens'.'

Pa looked serious.

'Maybe I should hitch up the buggy and come with you? Maybe me and the old man might deal better than you and him.'

Now those words amused me. I smiled tightlipped. No one was more explosive than my pa when he got his goolies in an uproar. I didn't want him fighting my battles, and maybe getting his fool head blown off. Any trouble and I was going to be in the front line my own self.

'You stay yourself right here with Jed and fort up. I don't want to come back here and find there's been a hunting party and the ranch afire. I'll tell Mickey to work within gunshot distance and you send for him and the boys pronto at the first sign of trouble.'

'You think the sheriff will let a posse come out here?'

'It wouldn't be legal if he wasn't heading it, but he's only one man and his deputy's only good for bouncing drunks. But if the mob get tanked up then anything could happen.'

'Right. I'll get the old shotgun down and cleaned up.'

I ate standing up and was soon on my way. I kept a good lookout for anything that moved but there was no sign of Tommy and Tabby. I knew in my heart they'd gone to their Grandpa Hitchens on account of Billy. What the hell they thought they could do, beat me. I couldn't see into their minds.

A couple of hours' hard riding and I neared their holding. I hadn't been nigh the place for years and saw that now it was a neat prosperous place with fruit trees carefully nurtured and a patchwork of cultivated fields. I drew rein at the top of the hill running down into the valley and surveyed the land. It was a fair sight and I could grudgingly admire the hard work gone into the development of the virgin land into this prosperous farm in the eighteen years since the Hitchens had come into our part of the world.

Then I put all good thoughts from me and concentrated on the mean and bitter part of me that had been forged willy-nilly by this hypocritical family who openly talked about the love of God, but brought up their children in soulless bigotry with their minds too narrow for the warmth of love.

At that moment I could nearly pity Amelia. She'd had no chance in that loveless household.

But now I had to concentrate on Tommy and Tabby. Were they down there pleading for Billy, with the mistaken idea they might be doing some good? I wondered briefly if I was to blame for all this. Had I been more seeing, more understanding, then maybe Tommy wouldn't have gone off half-cock to prove he wasn't a child no more, and as for Tabby … I'd never understand any of her motives, if I lived to be a hundred years.

I rode into the yard and hollered the house.

They took their time. Made me wait. I could feel eyes on me. I sat ramrod straight. I wasn't coming to beg.

Eventually, the white-bearded old man, his hair ruffled by the breeze came and leant up against the door jamb, a high-powered rifle balanced over his left arm. Maybe the stupid old fool thought I was going to shoot up the place!

'Ho there! I've come looking for my son and daughter. Are they with you?'

He took his time answering. He wanted to make me sweat. I felt mean. I looked mean but I waited.

'Yeh, they're here,' he finally answered slowly. 'They come to see their grandpa and grandma. Anything wrong in that?'

'Nope. If that be all they came for.'

'Why else should they come?'

'On account of Billy being set upon and took off to the town jail. You know anything about that?'

'Only what Tommy tells me. Wants me to intercede for Billy's release. I told him he must stand trial ....'

'No need for that, old man. He's free and back home where he belongs. Do you really think a boy of sixteen would kill Jesse Coates? Your own daughter's son?'

The old man looked down at this feet and then slowly put down the rifle so it leaned against the wall.

'Jesse Coates's foreman swore it was him. Everyone knows of the bad blood between him and DXL on account of the water rights.'

'But that don't mean a slip of a kid would do such a thing or that the truth was being told.

Maybe someone else wanted to stir up the townsfolk against the DXL outfit. Have you thought of that?'

Old man Hitchens looked up sharply, his eyes suddenly keen.

'Who would that be?'

'Coates's foreman himself. He's aiming to get married so I hear and old Jesse had no kith or kin and always treated his foreman as the son he never had. Maybe he wants the Coates place and the Drexel place too. It would be convenient if he ran us all off.'

That idea had just popped into my mind. It was hare-brained but the only idea I'd come up with. The more I thought of it, the more I liked the idea. After all, I was the only Drexel with know-how and strength. If Billy had got himself lynched that would have got me up and fighting and it would be easy to give me one in the back and then the two old men and Tommy and Tabby would have been sitting ducks.

Maybe I wasn't so far off the mark after all!

Old Hitchens was nearly as quick off the mark as me.

'Come in and let's talk about it.'

I shook my head. He might be kin of a kind, but I couldn't stomach visiting and maybe breaking bread.

'I've got to get back. I've just come for the kids.'

He nodded. 'I'll go get 'em.'

They came outside, looking a little shamefaced. Their grandma came too. She had a hand on Tabby's shoulder and Tabby looked a bit different and looking closer I saw her hair was shining and not in its usual rats'-tails. She was also wearing a fancy blouse instead of the usual man's check shirt. She looked quite pretty but it angered me. It was a reproach and I felt guilty.

'Come on, you two.' I said grimly. 'We've got some talking to do.' I didn't look at Martha Hitchens but turned my horse ready for home.

I heard Tabby thank her grandma for milk and cookies and for the blouse and I wanted to rip it off her. I kept silent until I heard them both trot up behind me.

We rode home in silence. I hoped they were sweating and worrying their guts like I'd been doing.

We were unsaddling the horses when Tommy said to me defiantly. 'We did it for Billy, Pa.'

'I know son, that's why I'm not giving you a leathering. It was a fool thing to do and you put Tabby at risk. Did you ever think you might run into the posse yourself?'

Tommy looked a bit staggered.

'No sir! I figured they'd go straight to Sweetwater and put Billy in jail.'

'You did, did you?' I snarled, suddenly furious.

'Somewhere they stopped long enough to beat your brother nearly to death! You'll see the results in the house. What do you think they might have done to your little sister?'

Tommy didn't answer but when we went indoors he maade straight for their bedroom. He looked down at Billy stretched out on his back, his face unrecognizable, his upper body black.

'They did this?' The face turned to me was that of an old man. 'I can't believe it, Pa. We've known most of those men since we were little nippers!' Billy groaned and opened his eyes at the sound of Tommy's voice.

'Hi, little brother. I thought I'd never see you again ....' He coughed as if his ribs hurt. I thrust Tommy aside.

'Your ribs hurting bad, Billy?'

He nodded. 'Then you need the doc. I'll send Mickey for him.' Then I remembered the widow-woman's words and decided to go myself. On the other hand, maybe I should do the persuading myself.

I drew Tommy out of the room. I could hear Pa talking and Tabby crying and knew she was getting a lambasting for rushing off. I looked at Tommy grimly.

'You've not heard the last of this boy, but for now you've got to help look after Billy while I ride for the doc. I think Billy's hurt inside and there might be more than just ribs!'

'Pa, I'm sorry. I just didn't like the idea of me not helping, especially when it was Billy ....'

'Well, you can help now. Look after Billy and keep an eye on Tabby while I'm gone.'

I punished my favourite mare that day. She was lathered and it washed all over me before we got to town. I called in at Pete's place and had me a drink to wash the dust out of my throat and then I hightailed it to the doc's. He wasn't in and an old woman sitting outside his door spoke up.

'You'll have a long wait, mister. He's celebrating the birth of Phil Harris's first baby. He's as drunk as a skunk!'

'Oh, yes? Well, he'll be as sober as if he was in church, when I catch up with him!'

I turned to make my way to the Stockman's Saloon, where all the elite of the town gathered and I bumped into Ruth Lowrie. I stepped back quick and touched my hat.

'Sorry, ma'am. I didn't see you there.'

She inclined her head and then said softly, 'How's Billy? He'll be in a lot of pain now the bruises are coming out.'

'Yeh. That's why I'm in town. I want the doc.'

She looked at the doc's shingle.

'I gathered that. You're wasting time, Mr Drexel. Believe me, the doc won't come. He's already made that quite clear.'

I looked her over, this six-foot bosomless woman with the bright chestnut hair screwed back into a bun which made her nose look too big for her face. She had a wide pleasant-looking mouth though, and her brown eyes had a twinkle and a compassion in them. I found myself thinking she wasn't quite as plain as I'd first thought. Her screwed-up hair and unflattering black widow's weeds made her appear older than she probably was. I summed her up as older than me and I was touching forty.

'Whatever his intentions were, ma'am, he's going to ride back with me to see Billy!'

I must have sounded pretty mean for she blinked.

'I'd like to see this, Mister Drexel. Doc Carruthers is a very determined man.'

'Well, if you're itching for excitement, just follow me, ma'am.' And I strode off, a little nettled at her attitude.

She had long legs under that black skirt and kept up with me and in her precise way kept up a flow of conversation which I scarcely heard. I was too intent on boning the doc and what I should do if the old cuss proved stubborn.

He wasn't only stubborn, he was filled with whiskey courage.

'Why should I come out to see a youth who should by rights be swinging from a rope?' he boomed, and then looked around at his listening cronies and grinned. I gritted my teeth.

'There's no evidence that he killed old Jesse and I'm not jawing about the whys and wherefores. You're coming with me!'

I made a move to collar him. He was a big man but he could move quick. His hand flashed to his side and I tried the old Indian trick of looking one way and kicking out with my foot in the other direction. I caught him a wallop in the groin.

He jack-knifed and I ran him, not too hard, against the saloon wall. I didn't want to addle his brains too much so that he couldn't do his job, but just enough to take the piss out of him. I succeeded. He came up like a lumbering bear, threw up a mess of whiskey and grub and then shook his head and peered at me through a mass of hair and whiskers.

'To hell with you! I'm not going out to the ranch,' he began belligerently. That was when I clocked him one where it would do the most good. He collapsed and groaned and then raised his head.

'I've got to think of my standing with the townsfolk. They can make or break me in this town, Drexel, and at the moment your name is shit!' There was a murmur in the crowd. I looked round at them all. Some who had been drinking buddies turned their heads away. I could have spat on them all. I took it out on the doc.

'Shit or not, you're coming with me!' I hauled him upright and slung him over my shoulder and he was no lightweight. I strode out of the saloon like all hell was after me, and not one of those watching protested.

I heard Ruth Lowrie say witheringly, 'I've never met so many men with yellow streaks up their backs! You're like a lot of sheep, listening to a lot of lies! Why don't you get off your arses and find the real killer of Jesse Coates?' Then she followed me at a gallop and coming alongside gasped, 'I've got my buggy handy. I'll drive him for you.'

My glance was wary. I wasn't used to females offering to do me favours ... I usually paid for what I got. She smiled a little.

'It's Saturday, if you're wondering how I've got free time.'

'No, ma'am, I wasn't wondering about your time but why you're willing to get involved.'

She went a little pink and her skin showed soft and unweathered, not like some of the hardcase women of the range that looked like fellers without the stubble.

'Do I have to have a reason? Let's say I don't like injustice. I've talked to my brother about what amounted to kidnap of your son and I know his views. He thinks it's ridiculous to put that murder on that boy and so do I!'

'And who does your brother blame for it then?

He must have some suspicions just as I have.'

She looked a little confused. 'I can't talk about what Joe thinks. It wouldn't be ethical.'

I'm not much good with the big words and I said as much.

'I sure don't know what it means, but I go along with you if you think so. You're one of those rare women who can keep her mouth shut.' Bless me, if her face didn't get as red as a turkey-cock's wattles! I couldn't figure why she should react in this way.

'Thank you, Mister Drexel. So I can drive the doctor? He looks to be in no condition to do it himself.'

'If you want to, I've no real objection,' I mumbled, 'but I could have hitched the mare behind ...'

'But it saves you the journey of bringing back the buggy,' she butted in and I didn't like to point out that the doc could have returned it. Women's reasoning was always illogical. Then I had a touch of inspiration.

'Mind you, it's on condition you call me Drex. Mister Drexel makes me feel uncomfortable.' And damn me if the woman didn't blush again!

She smiled and looked kind of pleased and I wondered why I'd thought her unattractive. It must be the screwed-up hair and the dowdy black.

So we moved out at a spanking pace, me aboard

the mare and her handling the reins on that buggy ride like an expert.

The first thing we did when we reached the ranch was strip the doc down to his breeches and shove his head in the horse trough. That brought him back to life faster than a racoon up his pants. He let out a Rebel yell that could be heard on our far distant range. Then Pa poured half a gallon of strong coffee down his throat that would have taken the silver plating off spoons, if we'd had any, never mind the skin of his throat.

While all this was going on, Ruth, followed by a mesmerized Tabby, did things in the sick-room and the upshot was that Billy was cleaned up and fed some nourishing beef broth and ready to be seen to by the doc when the old coot felt capable of doing his duty.

The result made me madder than a hornet. Those bastards had certainly turned the boy over good. He'd got damaged kidneys, a couple of broken ribs and his left cheekbone was cracked, along with sundry bruises and lacerations. He was now trussed up like a mummy.

The doc looked grave when he came from the room. Shaking his head, he said disbelievingly, 'If I hadn't examined him myself, I wouldn't have believed it possible the menfolk of Sweetwater Springs were capable of that kind of violence.' He looked me in the eyes, straight up. 'I'm sure ashamed to be one of 'em.'

I nodded and stuck out a fist.

'No hard feelings, Doc?'

'No.' He fingered his chin and grinned. 'You've got a hell of a punch, and if I'd been a young man I'd have been worried about pleasing the ladies. As it is ...' he shrugged, 'them days are long gone, but you sure left me sore!'

'Sorry about that, Doc. Do you want Mrs Lowrie to put some arnica on the place?'

For a moment he looked shocked. I laughed. It wasn't often one could shock a doctor! But he shocked me.

'I don't mind her doing the rubbing, but I sure as hell wouldn't have her put arnica on it! It's a damn delicate place is the groin. You have to treat it with respect!'

What could I say to that?

He was free to go and I expected Ruth Lowrie to go with him, but he stayed to jaw to Pa and Uncle Jed and they swapped yarns and nattered about the old days, and the doc recommended hot cow dung to plaster on to Uncle Jed's rheumatics and to lay off the liquor, which was ironic as the doc was filling up their glasses from Pa's store.

Finally we laid the old feller on a bunk. He was too paralytic to face the long ride back to town. For once, the good folk of Sweetwater Springs would have to do without their doctor. I hoped no babies were due.

Ruth Lowrie stared down at him, disapproval in every bone and muscle of her.

'He'll have a head like all getout, tomorrow.'

'Well, it's Sunday and he certainly livened up the oldsters. I've not seen them so perky for a long time.'

'They'll be bad too. You're going to have your hands full.'

'You think I can't cope? Tommy and Tabby will help me, so don't worry, I'll take you safely back to town. I'm going there anyway.'

'No, you're not! If you were counting on visiting Alice Symons, she's not there any more! She went off with a travelling salesman.'

'Well, I'm damned! After all these years, Alice actually caught a man!' Then I did a bit of thinking. 'How'd you know I'd be visiting Alice?'

'My God! Everyone in Sweetwater Springs knows you visited every Saturday night! You think we're all blind and deaf and five cents short of a dollar?'

I stared at her. Respectable women didn't talk like that. They weren't supposed to know about the dark side of a man's nature. She made me feel uncomfortable as if she could see right down into my dirty mean soul. I didn't like it. There were too many places there I didn't even like to see myself.

'Woman, you're the goldarnest, mouthiest most

shocking female I could have imagined! You shouldn't be talking to me about Alice Symons! A lady would never admit that she even existed!'

'I'm no lady and I must remind you I'm a widow, not some simpering young girl who doesn't know how many beans make five. I believe in speaking my mind ....'

'So I've noticed and you make a good job of it.'

'Then we know where we stand, don't we? Now as for me going back to town, I think Billy's condition is a good reason for me to stay.'

'Won't those God-fearing elders of Sweetwater Springs object to you staying overnight? After all, it's church funds that pays your wages as a teacher. You might pollute their young minds.' I spoke sarcastically. 'I would sure hate for you to lose your job.'

She lifted her head proudly and sparks flew out of those big brown eyes. She was a truly magnificent woman when roused. She made me think of warrior women defending their young.

'I don't give a damn for their opinion. I'm a good teacher and as far as they are concerned, my private life is my own. Not that I have much private life,' she finished forlornly, 'now that Ned is dead and gone.'

'I'm sorry.' I'm damned if I knew why I was sorry. She was making me uncomfortable again. Her mouth tightened.

'You know, being a female is most unfair, and do you know why?'

I shook my head. I'd never thought of women except in a carnal sense. I never stopped to think what went on in their heads.

'Then I'm going to tell you why, seeing as I like to put all my cards on the table.'

My lips twitched. I could just see her sitting playing poker and winning too ... and then her next words had me all agog and listening good and hard.

'You men can go out and have your fun whether it's womanizing or drinking yourselves silly and you're considered to be a good feller, a macho man and you get clapped on your back and you lose your gripes and urges. But a woman can't do any of these things. She restricted. If she marries, she takes on a man whatever he's like. She bears children and does her duty as a wife. She relies on him for every stitch of clothing, every bite she eats. She has no friends, except other women in the same position. Their lives are a dull round of feeding families, doing chores around the house and pretending to be happy.'

'Well, isn't that as it should be?'

'That's the way it is, not that it should be. If you're a spinster and don't have the good fortune to be either pretty or possessing a good dowry, then you're condemned to a life of good works and if you're lucky, a respected place in the church.'

'And what about widows? How are they expected to act?'

Now she had caught my attention in a big way. I sensed she was building up to something personal.

'Widows? They're the worst of the bunch. We're expected to mourn forever, no matter how young we are. We're neither fish nor fowl, with no man to defend us and we must rely on our relatives, whether we like it or not. Not a nice situation to be in, Drex.' She smiled a little as she saw my reaction to the use of my usual name.

'Is that so bad? Surely your life is as you make it, Ruth?'

For a long moment we looked at each other and I was conscious for the first time that I was a slovenly dresser and probably smelt, and I could do with a haircut.

Then her neatly flat bosom heaved as she forced herself to say defiantly, 'A widow has needs, Drex, just as a man has needs!' She didn't stop to see the effect of her words but turned on her heel and went into Billy's room.

I stood and stared at the slammed door with my jaw hanging nearly to the floor.

The doc opened one eye and looked up at me.

'You know, son, she's trying to tell you something. It's funny but human nature will out. She must have been frustrated for years!'

'But she's a schoolmarm, Doc! A pillar of the church!'

He grinned.

'But she'd rather be Alice Symons!'

I was outraged. She couldn't possibly have meant … could she?

THREE

It was a good thing Ruth and the doc stayed overnight. It was during the hour before dawn that Billy took a turn for the worse. Ruth, who'd been sleeping in the same room with Tabby beside her was soon at his bedside. He was in a high fever and when she roused the doc from his drunken stupor he pronounced him as being in the first stages of pneumonia.

It was then Ruth came into her own. She knew exactly what to do and with the doc's guidance brewed up poultices for his back and chest and made up a pungent concoction that stank but cleared his nasal passages.

Morning found us all red-eyed and anxious and when Mickey O'Rourke and the boys reported from the bunkhouse for breakfast and orders for the day, Ruth it was that coped with grub and brought order out of chaos.

One thing about Mickey, he was a man one could trust to get on with things. He just nodded when I gave him orders abruptly and after eyeing up Ruth speculatively, took the boys and went about the day's business.

Tommy and Tabby surprised me too. They fed the pigs and Tabby saw to the hens while Tommy carried water from the well and hauled in firewood. I didn't have to tell 'em anything. They just got on with the chores like the young troopers they were.

Sunday came and went and Doc stayed until Monday and then decided the crisis was over and Billy only needed good nursing.

I looked helplessly at Ruth. I couldn't bring myself to ask her to stay. It wouldn't have been right. The old gossips would have a field-day if she stayed behind. It was only Doc's presence that would save her reputation as it was. Besides, she had the school to run.

The doc climbed up on to Ruth's buggy and waited. Ruth looked at me and I looked at her. The doc coughed.

'Time's awasting, Mrs Lowrie. Are you coming or ain't yer?' and his tone was matter of fact. I don't think Doc Carruthers cared a shit about reputations.

She hesitated and swallowed and acted like some fool girl which was stupid seeing she was … how old … forty … forty-five?

'What should I do, Mister Drexel … Drex? The boy needs careful nursing but if I stay ….'

I nodded. 'I know. You'll be damned and finish up in hell!' I ground my teeth together and then I voiced what had been going through my mind all night. 'Why don't you move in as housekeeper and teach Tabby to be a young lady, and to hell with what those old besoms think in town?'

She hesitated.

'I've got my brother to think of, Drex. I'm his housekeeper and at least with him, I'm respectable!'

'God dammit! What d'you want? You'll be treated here with respect. What more can I say?'

She coughed delicately and the doc sighed.

'For the love of God, Drex, sharpen your wits! The woman's practically proposing so make up your mind. I'll have a queue a mile long waiting under my shingle!'

I blinked and she blushed and Tabby who'd just finished her chores, giggled.

I don't remember whether she ever did ask me proper, but the upshot was she stayed and the doc borrowed her buggy and went to town and no doubt spread the glad news to everyone he came in contact with.

There was no monkey business. The cabin wasn't big enough for that, besides I was shy of her. Fancy women and respectable women have a different aura around them. I still thought of Ruth as a being apart and I was in awe of her.

After a week and Billy was much better, we had time to really talk. I hadn't even given her a chaste kiss on the forehead. My heart failed me at the thought.

Sometimes at night in my lonely bed, I thought on her words when she talked about 'needs' but my mind boggled at what she might really mean. Somehow I couldn't picture her romping around as Alice Symons used to do.

We were still not visiting Sweetwater Springs but getting our supplies in Wichita and had planned to marry there when Billy was recovered and Ruth had promised that Tabby was to be a bridesmaid.

One thing I was pleased about and that was Tabby was much quieter these days, and didn't go flouncing off in unseemly rages. She and Ruth talked a lot and I saw her poring over a slate and make squiggly letters and I reckoned maybe I should buy some picture books when we hit Wichita.

Our talks didn't go down too well. I suppose we got to know each other better and I gradually got into a habit, like I did with Amelia, to wash more regular and shave. She was a good cook and we lived better and Pa and Uncle Jed approved my decision to marry and they thought I was a lucky dog.

I still wasn't sure whether I was doing right. I thought of Amelia lying like an icicle beside me and me having urges she wouldn't satisfy. It had been hell until I started visiting Alice. I didn't want all that hassle again.

Maybe I betrayed some of what was going through my mind.

It was her idea about ten days after she came to stay to ask me to take her riding so that she had some idea of what our ranges were like.

She was looking tired, what with all the strain of being up with Billy and looking after the household needs. I thought she deserved a break so told her to put a picnic together and we'd make a day of it.

I loaned her a pair of clean pants and one of my shirts and my best going-to-church, wide-brimmed hat. She looked kind of cute, if you can describe a tall woman like her, cute. She surprised me by being quite at home on horseback and then as we were riding along, told me that she and Ned used to go riding quite a lot when they were first married. He had been a lawman in a town about a day's ride beyond Wichita.

Then she told me about him being shot on a train by outlaws and how she'd come to look after her brother.

I'd found an ideal picnic spot after a few hours leisurely riding. We'd gradually ridden in the direction of our south border and I'd cast an eye over the fencing as we rode. We were not far from the J Bar C holding. There was a water-hole close by, one of those that had started the bad blood in the first place with Jesse Coates.

I helped her down, clasping her about the waist and noting the feel of her firm body under the shirt. Against my will, my blood quickened. I hadn't had the feel of a woman in weeks. We sat down not far from the spring which gurgled. There was rocks and foliage protecting us from the heat of the midday sun. We were quite cosy and the view was magnificent looking far down the valley where the dirt farmers had their holdings in one direction and our range dotted with cattle in the other direction.

I settled down to enjoy these brief hours and maybe really come to understand this woman a little better.

'How long were you married?' I asked. It seemed strange not to know anything at all about a woman I might just end up marrying if I could get the bugs out of my head.

'Five years,' she answered briefly, 'and yes, it was a happy marriage if you were thinking of asking.'

'Oh,' I said, daft like. She was quicker than me about these things. 'And how long have you been a widow?'

'Ten years come spring.'

'And you've worn black all this time?'

She sighed. 'What else could I do? I hate black, it brings back all the sorrow and heartache every single day of my life.'

'Then why endure it? Why not go into half mourning?'

'Because it was one of the conditions the church elders made when they offered me the job.'

'I wonder what those same elders think now, when you didn't return.'

She shrugged her shoulders. 'I'll have been consigned to hell!'

It was then I knew there was no going back. I couldn't change my mind about marrying her. I couldn't be that kind of bastard to her.

She looked challengingly at me. I think she knew what was in my mind. Then she surprised me.

I watched as she slowly unbuttoned that check shirt and I gulped when I saw she'd shed the usual fal-de-lals women wear under their clothes. She pulled down the pants I'd given her and damn me, she was bollack naked! I couldn't believe my eyes and I was more than a mite shocked, respectable women are supposed to be armour-plated around their nether parts.

'Well? Don't you want to try before you buy?'

And damn me, I was like a boy on his first fumble!

Then pulling myself together, I thought of Alice and what she found pleasureable and thought, in for a cent, in for a dollar! So I gently took off the shirt and looked at her white skin and the flat chest which now didn't seem so flat but crowned with pink roseate peaks and boy, were they peaking!

I could hardly tear my eyes away from her pulsating softness but when I did, I saw her eyes all lit up and eager for me. Then for me, the screwed-up hair jarred as it reminded me she was a schoolmarm, and I unpinned all that brightness and her hair flowed down her shoulders like a copper cloud all wavy and twisty curls.

I ran my fingers through it. She was another person, more vulnerable, more feminine.

Then I was burying my face in all that softness, breathing in the sweet smell of her and I found myself kissing every inch of that petal-soft skin.

I got the biggest shock however, when she finally wound those long shapely legs around my buttocks. She was athletic, and boy, did she make up for ten years of widowhood!

There was no more heartsearching about marriage. I was willing to be leg-shackled anytime! I wanted her permanent, and woe betide the man who might stop me having her!

Later, I watched her drag her hair back into its customary bun, with no hint of wave or curl, and I was pleased and made up my mind she'd always wear it that way, for no man would suspect the real woman as I now knew her. Ruth, with hair about her shoulders and passionate, was for me alone, I'd kill the man who looked at her with lust in his eyes ....

I was startled at these thoughts. I'd never been jealous of Amelia. I didn't know I was capable of such deep uncompromising jealousy. Ruth had brought me alive this bright morning.

We faced each other as we ate our picnic and drank the coffee I'd brewed. I was happy and it was a strange feeling. I'd never felt this way before.

Afterwards, we sat together watching the dying fire and talking of our future together and I was amazed when she said she was thirty-six years old and hoped we should have children. I kind of thought it was diplomatic not to tell her I'd estimated her age to be in the forties. Women are usually sensitive about age.

I thought of Billy and Tommy and Tabby and wondered whether she would act up like Amelia once she'd got her babies and I thought it right that I should speak up and say what was in my mind.

She laughed when I told her about Amelia but there was sympathy for me in her eyes as she laughed.

'I'm no Amelia. I wasn't brought up in a loveless household where godliness of spirit was put before Ma's physical needs. My parents were a loving kindly couple who gave Joe and me all the support and love we needed. My sorrow was that Ned and I never had children. I could have had children the same age as yours if God had willed it.' She sounded sad and wistful. My heart went out to her and I took her hand palm up and kissed it, all gallant like.

'Honey, I'll do my level best to get you in the family way, I promise you.' And we laughed together and I couldn't believe my good luck in finding such a woman.

The sun was going down when we finally made a move, and so we left our cosy nest amongst the bushes and the rocks and we started our leisurely ride home following our boundary fences so that I could check it as we went.

We'd come to the top of a rise and drew rein to give the horses a breather and to admire the views right along the Sweetwater Valley. A magnificent sunset streamed across our range causing dark shadows that made trees and boulders stand out sharply against the sky.

Suddenly I was conscious of a sound all stockmen dread, the drumming of hooves of a stampeding herd. I cursed. Ruth looked at me sharply.

'What is it, Drex?'

'Stampede, and going away from us in that direction.' I pointed to the Sweetwater Valley. To see what was going on I had to ride a fair ways and then climb an escarpment. It was imperative I should know just what was going on. Those could be my cows down there ....

'You stay here and I'll go take a look.'

'I'm coming too, Drex.'

This was no time for argument and I already knew she could be a stubborn woman.

She followed me up that escarpment like a monkey. Gasping, we watched about a hundred cows of ours go pouring through a gap in the fence and on to J Bar C land, and behind them were at least six cowboys that I could see. So this was a deliberate act of rustling!

'See that! The bastards have deliberately cut my fence and driven the cattle through! I'll have their balls! I'll skin 'em alive. I'll ....' And then I stopped. For a moment I'd been so dammed angry I'd forgotten she wasn't one of the boys. 'I'm sorry, I let myself be carried away.'

'It's all right! I'm old enough to have heard it all before and much worse, and believe me I've been known to use bad language on occasion.' I gave her a quick kiss and then I really let rip as we watched the efficient way those cattle were being driven.

Back at the ranch we went into a huddle. Pa

and Uncle Jed were for going all out to the J Bar C ranch and shooting everyone up as in the old days. Mickey O'Rourke said we should backshoot the bastards and go get our cows.

I was more cautious now I'd had time to think. I wanted nothing illegal to happen. We were in deep enough shit as regards Billy and the ludicrous charges laid against him. So I gave orders for the fence to be repaired and a section left to be lifted aside as a gate when we drove our cattle back again.

I was going to have those cattle back, come hell or high water, and our visit next day would determine how we should get 'em.

So early next morning we saddled up and went on the long trek to the J Bar C ranch. Ruth had been up since four o'clock fixing grub for all of us, no mean feat for more than a dozen healthily starving men.

She waved goodbye and I had a lump in my throat. It was times like these when it brought it home to me how lonely I'd been all these years.

Tommy appeared all bleary-eyed just before we moved off. Silly young fool wanted to come with us without even having his breakfast. He was wanting to grow up too fast, and being small and skinny as against Billy's huskiness, he'd always hated himself and wanted to prove something, and I hadn't the sense to understand it was me he wanted to prove himself for.

We rode hard, Mickey and me, and the boys in twos behind us like in the cavalry in the old days. As we rode we talked tactics and I described what happened.

'It was a deliberate act of rustling.'

'And why do you think he did it, boss? He must surely know we'd come looking.'

'To cause an incident, Mickey. Tad Grainger's got big ideas now that he's boss of the J Bar C. He goaded Jesse on to battle for our water in the old days. Pa and Jesse were good friends until Tad Grainger came on the scene. He's a bad man to cross, is Tad Grainger.'

And so we found, when we finally rode into the J Bar C yard and hollered the house. Tad Grainger's answer was a warning shot. The boys scattered but I stood my ground despite a rearing horse who wanted to bolt.

'What you want?' growled Tad Grainger as he stepped outside his door with a shotgun at the ready. It looked mighty like he was expecting us, for as I looked around I saw his men at strategic points amongst the barn and buildings and all had guns cocked and ready for use.

'We're looking for strays,' I replied evenly, mentally counting the opposition and realizing the bastard had all his men to hand, and none out on the range. We was outnumbered.

'I seen no strays. Have any of you boys seen any DXL steers?'

Somebody laughed. I didn't like that.

'No, boss,' Tad Grainger's foreman sang out. Again someone guffawed. I whirled about.

'If any of you know anything, spit it out loud and clear or I'm going to be accusing someone of rustling!'

'That's fighting talk, Drex,' Grainger drawled. 'I'm entitled to defend my good name if you persist.'

'I do persist, mister. Last night some of my cows were driven on to your land and by your men. Do you deny it?'

'Of course I deny it but if you're so goddamned sure, why say you've come looking for strays?'

'To save a range war, mister. I was wanting to give you a chance. As it is, I want my riders to ride your range and cut out all DXL steers and we'll say no more about it. After all, we're neighbours, and the way I see it, even a vulture wouldn't shit so near home!'

Tad Grainger looked angry and for one minute I thought he was going to blast me with the shotgun. I braced myself, and I got the old twitchy feeling in my trigger finger. I think he remembered just in time that years ago I'd been a trigger-happy young hellion and could still do some fancy shooting.

'You can save your breath and energy. None of your steers are mixed with mine.'

He sounded so damn positive that if I hadn't actually seen the drive myself I'd have believed him. As it was, I was having doubts.

'Maybe you have, maybe you ain't, but my boys are taking a looksee and I warn you, if they find those cows, there's going to be hell to pay in the Sweetwater Valley!'

He laughed.

'Go ahead. Search until you've got blisters on your arses! You'll find none.' He stumped back into the house, a giant of red-headed bloody-mindedness.

He was right. We found no trace of DXL cattle and at last Mickey O'Rourke lifted his sweaty hat and wiped his forehead.

'You sure about what you saw, boss? It might have been their cattle they herded back.'

'I'm sure. I saw the old Mexican bull with the curly horns leading his harem. Nobody, unless he was blind, could mistake that bunch with those distinct markings. Anyhow, if some of his were amongst them, why not admit it and then mend the fence instead of leaving it as if the cattle had bust their way through?'

Mickey shrugged heavy shoulders.

'Then how come we find no DXL's?'

'There's some devilry afoot, you can bet your

best saddle on it.'

Tad Grainger watched us depart and there was a grin on his face I should have dearly liked to wipe off the hard way. But I could wait and watch. I'm a patient man when necessary. I had a distinct feeling that all this was tied up with Jesse's murder and Grainger's ambitions to own all the range.

We were a hungry lot who arrived back long after dusk. Ruth, bless her, had the great black iron pot of stew simmering away on a trivet and by the smell that greeted us at the door, she'd got oven fresh bread ready to sop up the gravy.

We tucked in good and she topped up the meal with huge helpings of dried apricot pie. The boys loved it. I joked that she should give Uncle Jed some lessons in cooking.

'Why?' she asked outright in front of everyone. 'I thought it would be my job in the future.'

So of course, to the cheers and the catcalls from the boys, I found myself committed, burnt my boats for good and all.

Billy was up now, his bruises disappearing, his chest easier and only his ribs giving him gyp. It would be a week or two yet before he could ride again. I was worried however. We could still get a visit from a posse come looking for the boy, especially if they couldn't find the real murderer.

However, it hadn't occurred to the boy that he

might still be in the running for the noose, but was looking happy about Ruth becoming part of the family. He'd had a good opportunity to get to know her in these last few days. I was pleased.

There was no aggravation from Tommy and certainly none from Tabby as she'd run after Ruth ever since she'd arrived and it brought it home to me how much these kids had missed out on having a ma.

Tabby flung her arms about my neck and embarrassed me by giving me several kisses all buried in my beard. She beamed at me.

'I was hoping Ruth would stay with us, Pa. I like her a lot!'

Pa grinned and Uncle Jed scratched his bristly chin.

'I always hated doing the cooking. I always said I'd rather chop wood.' Then he too grinned and stretched out a grimy paw and shook my hand.

Then it was up to me and I got a good grip of Ruth and gave her a hearty smacker on her cheek. After that it was business as usual.

And the business came faster than we expected and from quite another source.

The boys had gone off to do their usual chores and left only the two oldsters, the kids and Ruth and me and so we all watched the bunch of riders making for our yard.

It was Ruth who whipped down the first rifle

from the wall rack and held it out silently to me. Pa and Uncle Jed followed suit.

I thought of Billy and the Sweetwater jail and like hell would I let him be taken.

But it wasn't Billy they were after. It was me.

I stepped on to the veranda with the old Spencer at the ready. They were strangers excepting for Ned and Bob Hitchens, and they sure had to have their nebs into every bit of business.

'You Hal Drexel?' The man speaking was evidently the leader. He was dressed shabby in canvas pants and torn shirt and wore no hat and his hair was long and wild, like some hillbilly.

'Speaking, and who might you be?'

'I'm Moxy Somers and me and these here fellers represent the farmers from down the valley. We're here to tell you that we're moving in. A lot of this land' – he looked about him – 'is free range and we've got a right, especially as you let your cattle eat their way through our crops!'

'You lie! My stock is fenced in!'

'Then how come there's DXL cattle all over my fields and none of your cowboys in sight?'

'Ah ...!' So that was what happened to those cows! My mind worked furiously and I remembered that strip of ground running like a panhandle next to the J Bar C holdings. The bastards had cut across his own land and turned those cows into that strip of land and offloaded them on to Somers' cultivated fields.

The sly bastard!

I could see it all. Start off the aggravation and let the farmers do the dirty work and while we got all fired up with each other, he, Tad Grainger, would step in!

Moxy Somers was looking grim as he watched my reactions.

'There's no use thinking up excuses, Mister Drexel. We've had cattle roaming before and always turned 'em back without complaining, but now it's gone too far. Those cattle of yours have wrecked my entire harvest. What you going to do about it?'

'What can I say? I didn't even know there's been a spate of straying. This is all news to me, Mister Somers.'

'You're a lying dog! I've watched your cowboys come before and herd 'em away, but this time was different. You left 'em deliberate on my best field of alfalfa. Are your pastures bad you can't feed up your cows?'

I was beginning to lose my temper but felt Ruth's hand warningly on my arm.

'Ask him how long it's been going on, Drex,' she whispered and I bawled out the question.

The men behind him were growing restive and now the Hitchens brothers eased their horses forward.

Ned, the oldest brother, brushed Somers aside.

'Here, let me deal with him, Moxy. He's a hard man and one to watch. I know. He made life hell for my cousin Amelia.' I heard the words distinctly and I wanted to rush at him and drag him off his horse and shove his lying tongue down his throat and push his head up his arse.

'I'm asking again. How long has this been going on, Somers?'

'What's it matter how long it's been going on?' snarled Ned Hitchens. 'The point is, it's happened and not only to Somers but to the rest of us. All of us have suffered from your damned cattle, haven't we fellers?' He looked round at the rest of them. They all nodded looking grim.

'It matters to me. Have you been having trouble since old Jesse was backshot?'

There was silence and they all looked at each other. Ned lifted his hat and scratched his bald pate and Bob nudged him and said something in a low tone.

Then Moxy Somers spoke up.

'You might say the trouble started round about that time. What of it?'

'Because I don't think old Jesse would have let our cows through to stray down the valley. We was at loggerheads about water rights, but he sure wouldn't have allowed a dirty trick like that, especially when his own stock could have become mixed in. Was there any J Bar C stock wandering down the valley?'

'Come to think of it, there weren't which is strange,' Moxy Somers looked surprised. He hadn't thought of that before.

'What the hell matters about whose stock it was,' Ned Hitchens butted in rudely. 'It's done and we want to know what you're going to do about it. Our crops are ruined, our irrigation channels trampled ....'

'I'll tell you what I'm going to do,' I shouted, real mad by this time. 'I'm going to find out who killed Jesse and when I do that, I'll know who's behind this aggravation and I tell you now, I've got a bloody good idea ....' Ruth's warning nip on my bicep stopped me going further. 'Now get to hell off my land and stay off if you know what's good for you.' I aimed a shot above the heads of the bunch at a lone bird flying by and he fluttered down, a tumbling scattered mass of feathers.

'We've not come to an arrangement,' Ned Hitchens began.

I shut him up with a shot that tweaked his hat from his head. He turned without a word and started to trot away.

I stopped him with a stentorian shout.

'Take your louse-infected hat with you! I don't want it polluting my ground!'

He scooped it up and after looking at the hole in the crown, jammed it firmly on his head and rode away without looking back.

FOUR

It was time to go hunting. I slammed my way back into the house, pushing Ruth to one side as she tried to restrain me. I reached for a box of cartridges and loaded up and then checked my guns, and for the first time in years strapped two down to my thighs. I was going on the prod.

'What are you going to do?' Ruth gasped and looked from me to Pa and Uncle Jed. They both looked away from her. They knew what had to be done. This was man's business.

Tommy was looking white and put an arm about Tabby. I could see he was concerned for me. Billy disconcerted me by appearing unmoved. It came to me that perhaps I'd always favoured the wrong son. Maybe I'd been unfair because Tommy had been the small sickly son. Courage came in all kinds of parcels. It was a lesson to ponder over when I had the time.

Now, I could only get to figuring how and when I was going to corner Tad Grainger and beat the the truth out of him.

I ran down the steps of the veranda and rang the dinner bell and soon Mickey O'Rourke and several of the boys working within earshot of the bell, gathered in the yard.

'We've had callers.' I told what had happened and how I meant to hunt up Tad Grainger and get the truth out of him. 'So as it's not your fight, I'll not hold it against anyone not wanting to follow me.'

Old Solly Jones who'd been with Pa since he was a lad, spoke up for all.

'What affects DXL affects us all. This is our home ground. Isn't that right fellers?'

They all made suitable noises so without more ado, we saddled up and when we were ready I lifted my hat to Ruth and gave the kids a brief wave and we were off.

We headed for the J Bar C ranch but met Luke, our wrangler, leading in a lame horse he'd found straying. When he heard what was on he figured to come with us, but, he said, Tad Grainger was on course for town with some of his riders. He'd seen 'em pass near the old Indian trail not an hour ago.

So Luke saved us the long haul to the J Bar C ranch and we headed across country towards Sweetwater Springs and some two hours later we rode into town, me and Mickey in front and eight riders spaced out across the road leading down Main Street.

We came in cautious and steady and the townsfolk must have sensed trouble in the air for they all scattered, even the dogs scuttled under floorboards and peeped out to watch what was going on.

We dismounted in front of the Stockman's Saloon and I punched open the batwing doors and strode inside, guns jumping into my fists like in the old days before I knew what fear was.

The room was half full, the once rich furnishings grimy from the hazy blue smoke that never cleared. The place stank of stale beer and cheap scent from the fancy women who hung around any man who sported a roll of bills. Two tables, alongside the fancy bar, were being used for poker and I saw that Tad Grainger and some of his cronies were playing and that Tad sat with his back to the wall and his gun was standing by.

He leaned forward as I entered, chewing on a cigar. He waited. Watchful.

The small crowd parted like they said the Red Sea did in the Bible.

'Tad Grainger, we're going to have this out once and for all. I want to know just how Jesse Coates died.'

'You've got a nerve, coming in here like this, when everyone knows your boy did it!'

'You're a liar! Billy wasn't even in town when it happened.'

'I saw him and my word is good enough for the citizens of this here town and when we get a judge here, we're gonna up and take him, so help me!'

My hands twitched. Once upon a time I'd never even have let a man spit, never mind give me all this bullshit. But now age had made me wary. I could be digging my own grave.

'They'll want more than your word. You'll want witnesses ....'

'Oh, I've got them, make no mistake, I've got that boy of yours sewn up right and tight. It's just a matter of doing it all legal like. We've got the noose all ready!'

'Why you bastard ....' I drew my guns and as I fired, he kicked the poker table over and my slugs tore splinters out of it. Then all hell broke loose and the boys behind me let rip and the famous mirror behind the bar which had taken Billy Mundy so long to install, shattered into a thousand shards.

The women screamed and were tossed to one side like fading flowers, while those who were not involved in our dispute struggled to get out of one of several doors into the yard.

I caught a slug in the soft part of my upper arm. It stung but hadn't done much damage. I went hunting for Grainger. He'd somehow crawled away under cover of the first blast. I cursed, and as some of my boys began some infighting and settling old scores, I eased myself out of the mob and went into the yard looking for the red-headed giant.

A small frightened boot boy peeked out at me from behind a rain barrel.

'Looking for someone, mister?'

'Aye, a big man with red hair.'

'You mean, Mister Grainger?'

'Yeh, that's him. Where did he go?'

'Tossed me half a dollar to open the stable door and shut it again after he was gone. He took off out of town, mister.' He held his hand out. I gave him a dollar. The kid had all his buttons on.

I raced around the building, but there was no sign of the lying bastard. He'd got away. I went back inside and the fighting had cooled a little but not without some damage to the building. Someone had catapulted over the bannister going up the stairs and I guessed it was Mickey for he had a glazed look in his eyes and a splinter of wood in his ear lobe and much blood coursing down his shoulder.

He laughed at my look of enquiry.

'It was a rickety stairway in any case, and Tad Grainger's foreman tried to get away via the girls' rooms. One of 'em screamed a warning and I up and went after him. We came down together but I was on top. He's over there in the corner and I'm afraid he won't remember much of this here little party!'

'Neither will the barman, by the look of him. I think this calls for the doc. I hope the old bugger makes them pay through the nose for his services.'

Gradually the mayhem died away. We had a couple of fellers with shotgun wounds as well as myself, and there were sundry cuts and bruises for the good doc to tend to. Mind you, he upped his charges and the whole schemozzle cost me a sight of money which I reluctantly paid seeing as the boys laid their lives on the line for me.

It taught me a lesson. Not to go in ham-sam, fists flying and guns roaring. I would have to catch Tad Grainger in another way, something that would be personal to just us two and not to have the boys involved.

We rode back to the ranch, a sorry bunch and most of us bandaged in some place or other, with Sheriff Tomlin's words ringing in our ears.

'Don't be a fool, Drex. Next time you go shooting up the Stockman's Saloon might be your last. Grainger was waiting for you, no doubt about that. You got off light because he didn't figure you'd bring your boys. We both know that boy of yours is being set up but it's proving it, Drex. I've no more idea how it was done than you do, but the fact remains, Jesse was gunned down behind the Stockman's Saloon and as he wasn't no drinker as such, and too old to be sniffing after the women, then why was he there in the first place?'

That got me thinking. Why had the old man been in that place and late at night?

I thought about it all the way back to the ranch. There was an answer to that and as like as not it was staring me in the face.

I missed Ruth as soon as I walked in the door. There was a smell of burnt stew like when Uncle Jed did the cooking. I looked about me as I unbuckled my gunbelt and threw it down on the settle. My arm ached and my arse was blistered with riding and I was in no fit state to start figuring what was up.

I looked at Pa in his usual chair by the fire and then at Uncle Jed in his sacking apron.

'That apron's disgusting. What you been doing? Wiping the pig's arse with it? Wait till Ruth sets eyes on you. Where is she?' I spat out the last words real mean. I also registered that Tabby hadn't come running which was unusual. 'And where's Tabby for Christ's sake? You've not let her run wild while we've been away?'

Pa cleared his throat and spoke up. 'We thought they'd come back with you.' I saw his glance at Uncle Jed who frowned.

'What d'you mean, come back with us? Where

the hell did they go?'

Uncle Jed butted in. 'Now Drex, take it easy. Ruth figured that if you were going over to the J Bar C it was a good time for her to go home and get a few duds and talk to her brother and go and face the reverend, and tell him to stuff his job. Tabby wanted to go with her and they were going to buy stuff for a dress for Tabby, seeing as she's always made do with Tommy's castoffs. Tabby wants to be a girl. Is there any harm in that?' His voice tailed away as he saw my grim look. 'What is it, Drex?'

'I'll tell you what it is! They never arrived in Sweetwater Springs! I was talking to her brother and Ruth never went home! Another thing, we didn't go the J Bar C, we headed for town seeing as Grainger and his boys had gone there!'

There was a shocked silence before Pa erupted into a blazing rage mouthing curses I'd never even heard of before. I thought he was going to have a heart attack.

'Stop it!' I bawled at the top of my lungs. 'For God's sake, calm down, we don't want to have to dig another grave out there before time, do we? Now take hold of yourself and sit down and take a slug out of that bottle you've got hid behind your chair!'

With Pa calmer, I turned to Uncle Jed.

'Give me some of that revolting stew of yours

and I'll go look for them.'

'You can't, man. You're all washed up! You'll have to wait until tomorrow.'

'And leave Ruth and Tabby at the mercy of that man? He must have had them hogtied all along even as we had that shootout. How he must have laughed to himself about it! No wonder he was good and ready! He'd figure we knew then that he'd got them! Give me that stew.'

Uncle Jed served me the stew. It wasn't bad, just a bit smoked and I was hungry enough to eat cowpats. I dunked some of Ruth's stale bread into the gravy and filled up the hollows. Belching a little, I drank coffee laced with whiskey and I was ready to face Grainger again.

I was saddling up when I saw Billy and Tommy coming from the bunkhouse. Billy was moving easier but Tommy still had to help him walk. It passed through my mind that Tommy was growing up fast and using his initiative. He could use his head. I was beginning to think that Billy was going to be all brawn with not too much on top. Not that it would matter in the long run. I was proud of them both. I just didn't have time to tell 'em.

I put them in the picture and rode off. Both boys stood and watched me but I could see that Billy was quite prepared to let me go. Maybe he trusted me more to keep out of trouble. Tommy, on the other hand, looked worried and I don't think it was just on account of the womenfolk.

I checked my rifle in the boot strapped to the mare and then eased the guns in their holsters which rested comfortably on my thighs. I was ready for action wherever it came from, for I had a spine-tingling suspicion that Grainger would have some hidden lookouts dotted around the approaches to his ranch.

I was still caught short. A slug zoomed past my head as I moved from my land to his. It came from a line cabin I had to pass on the way. The mare's stride lengthened instinctively and saved me from the second shot. I whipped up an incline and as we passed a jumble of rocks I vaulted from the saddle and the mare went galloping on, reins tossing free.

Whoever was shooting at me must have thought he'd got me when he saw the horse galloping by because the door opened and a dark figure stepped out. I caught him in the shoulder and he spun around with a piercing cry and toppled over and rolled quite a ways before striking his head on a rock and lying still.

He'd have a nasty headache for a day or two.

I whistled for the mare and she came running, and after that little episode I took more care and time and kept away from the usual trail to cross the J Bar C land. I approached the buildings from the back side, and halted the mare just below the skyline so that I could watch any activity below.

It was dusk and in an hour it would be dark. I studied the layout of the buildings, which was the barn, the cookhouse and the bunkhouse and the blacksmith's shop. All were potentially dangerous. I could hear laughing coming from the bunkhouse. Whoever was stationed as lookout did not reveal himself with a cigarette. I had no way of knowing where watching eyes could follow my movements.

I sat in the dark, figuring out where Grainger would keep Ruth and Tabby. I was in no doubt that they were to be his bargaining tools. I knew what he wanted and he knew I knew. I looked back over the years when a reluctant Jesse Coates had come to Pa and offered to buy him out because he wanted a larger spread.

In those days the old man had a lifetime's savings to back him up. Later, he'd become belligerent, threatening and making out that the water rights was the real trouble. Now I knew different. That old man had been under pressure from Grainger for I calculated it all had started from when Tad Grainger had come to him as an ambitious youth.

The old man must have resisted some. Maybe more than we realized. Because, no doubt about it, in the early days, Jesse had been a good friend to Pa. It all boiled down to Grainger having some hold over Jesse and the old fool hadn't been able to bring himself to confide in anyone.

So he'd got backshot for his pains.

It would have been interesting to go see the land records up at the county seat. All this speculation led me think that Tad had somehow got old Jesse to make the place over to him before his murder. After all, there were rumours that Tad Grainger was sparking Miss Charlotte Pierce, the reverend's daughter. Now *that* was enough to make Grainger make a move.

So figuring all this out made me think that he'd treat Ruth and Tabby good. After all, he wouldn't want to do anything criminal or it would explode any hope of marrying Miss Charlotte.

I took heart and got me moving and I bellied down and covered the ground slow and easy. There was a bit of a moon but it was cloudy in fits and starts. There was a chill wind and a smell of rain to come. I hoped I wouldn't be in the midst of a deluge before this night was over. I still hadn't figured on how to get them away when I'd freed them. I should have had sense to bring horses, a cumbersome task when one wanted to ride fast.

I reached the ranch and ran crouching down and taking a quick peep round corners before proceeding further. Then I detected smoke and knew someone was outside smoking a cheroot. I watched and saw a movement of shadow across the front yard and behind a woodpile. So I'd located the lookout.

It had to be Josh Morton, who was Grainger's lickarse. He would do any dirty job if he was paid well enough. Maybe he'd been the one to pull the actual trigger when Jesse got shot.

I made a detour and came up behind him. I collared him around the neck in the crook of my arm and dragged him back over. He nearly swallowed his cheroot.

'Make a sound, little man, and I'll choke you to death,' I whispered in his ear. He gurgled and I drew him well away from the house. Then I let him have it, a sharp rabbit chop that put his lights out for the next few hours. I left him snoring heavily behind the blacksmith's shop as being the safest place.

Then I crept back Indian fashion and watched and listened. No one had missed him and nothing stirred, not even a dog came prowling.

So I took me a risk and looked in the only lighted window and there they were, Ruth, with an arm about Tabby sitting together on a horsehair sofa near a blazing log fire and Tad Grainger standing in front of them. He had a glass in his hand and appeared to be toasting them. I wondered why.

Tabby was frightened. Even through the

window I could see the marks of tears, but Ruth sat proud and stubborn and I thanked God for that same stubborness. Tad Grainger wouldn't have the satisfaction of listening to her pleading.

The rage within me, I'd managed to control with an effort as I had waited. But now seeing them, and Tabby's fear, made the rage burst into flame and I was reckless, unheeding. I drew the two Colts and turned to go and kick in the door and came face to face with the biggest, most powerful black man I'd ever seen.

It was the last thing I knew, for a black fist, like ebony, connected to my chin and the world exploded.

I came back to life trussed up like a side of beef ready for spitting. Ruth and Tabby were still on the sofa and I swivelled myself around and saw that they were roped. The movement I made alerted Grainger who came and looked down at me and grinned.

'So you haven't a glass jaw. I thought Ely had killed you and that would sure upset my plans.'

My head sang and my jaw hurt like all get out when I tried to speak.

'And just what are your plans?' I managed to ask.

'I think you know the answer to that, Drexel. I want the DXL and I want it quiet and discreet. I aim to be someone in this community and I want it to be soon. You and yours can go if you sign a agreement to sell to me at my figure. Oh, I'll not leave you penniless, Drexel. I'm not really a bad man.' He smiled. 'I'm aiming to get the power of the Lord around me, so I don't want to do no killing, not when I intend to become the Reverend Pierce's son-in-law. You understand me, Mrs Lowrie? Just you persuade Drex here to be sensible.'

'And what if I won't persuade him, Mr Grainger?'

'Then you'd be a very foolish woman, Mrs Lowrie, but I don't think I'd reckon you to be so foolish!'

'You would never get away with it!' Ruth spoke strongly. By God, she was magnificent!

'I can get away with anything I like. No one knows you're here and this fool' – he kicked me in the ribs – 'has never been here. Right?'

'That's where you're wrong, Grainger. My family know where I was heading! They'll come hunting if I don't show up!'

'Oh, they'll find you all right. They'll not come hunting to the J Bar C, for they'll find you on your own land, fallen from a convenient butte, maybe … or perhaps with a broken neck and your horse lame from stepping into a hole. There's a lots of ways of setting up an accident.'

Then I opened my mouth and put my foot

straight into the quagmire, I was that stark staring, fighting mad.

'It's no good, Grainger we know you killed old Jesse personal. You had him come into town to see Jessop at the bank and draw up his will. We also know he turned his place over to you. It's all there to be seen at the Land Records office in Wichita. You had the motive and you had the opportunity.'

I watched as he gave a start of surprise and knew I was on to something. It had started as a bluff, my mind working overtime and I don't really know why it all came out pat. But I'd struck a chord and I twanged it for all it was worth.

He let me have my say, a peculiar smile twisting his mouth as I hammered home what I was sure was the truth of it. I was blind to the dangers of Ruth and Tabby, only thinking in that blind moment about Billy and getting him off the hook.

I was a fool, good and proper and it was Ruth who pulled me up sharp.

'Drex! For God's sake.! Don't you see? He'll not let any of us go now, no matter how much I persuade you. He can make you sign anything he likes ....'

'She's right, Drex. I can take my time with you, or ...' and now he laughed in a high-pitched crazy way as if all control was leaving him; he was on an ego trip, 'we could start with the kid. I don't think you'd like to see her suffer, would you, Drex?'

'You fiend! This is between you and me, Grainger. Leave Tabby out of it. Let her and Ruth go, and we'll talk terms.'

'I think that's too late, Drex. Mrs Lowrie has a shrewd head on her shoulders and she can face reality. I think I'm going to have to have a talk with your old man, Drex. He should prove much easier to persuade to leave. You've still got two sons he'll want to protect!'

I didn't answer. I was thinking of my two guns which had been taken from me and thrown on to the blackwood dresser. If I could only get to them ....

I braced myself and then suddenly bunched both legs and lashed out and caught Grainger on the kneecaps. My wrists were tied but I was in a position to mash the bastard's face to a pulp. He jack-knifed forward and I caught him a cracker with my heels. I heard the bone in his nose crack, and he fell on top of me, blood drenching my front. I bit his ear. He screamed.

Then he was scrambling away from me and clawing for his gun and suddenly the door burst open and a white-faced Tommy was straddling the opening and he was hanging on to Pa's old shotgun and he let whizz and the shot peppered the back wall like as if giant woodlice had attacked it.

I think Grainger either fainted with the shock

of the attack or else I'd caught him proper in the goolies for he was lain prone and I was soaking up his blood.

Tommy nearly cut my hands off as he jabbed at the cords binding my wrists. He was so upset, his hands trembled. I cut the cords binding my ankles myself to be on the safe side. Then I joined Tommy as he sawed away at Tabby's bonds.

'Always remember to carry a well-honed knife, Tommy, or you might do more damage when you're saving someone!'

It was a poor attempt at a joke but he took me seriously.

'I hope I don't have to save anyone else. Pa. I don't like the excitement.'

'No … well, you still want a sharp knife. You never know what you might need it for.' He grinned and I slapped him on the back. Then I turned my attention to Ruth and Tabby and I hugged them close and I'm not ashamed to say it, but I cried.

There was no sign of the big black feller. Evidently Grainger had told him to buzz off, not wanting him to know all his affairs with us of the DXL, which was a mistake on Grainger's part and good for us.

But I got the biggest surprise outside. Billy was there, propped up on the seat of Ruth's buggy. He looked a little pale and he was sweating, evidently his broken rib was still giving him gyp. But he was manfully hanging on to Uncle Jed's favourite hunting rifle and looked ready to blaze away at anything that stirred.

He gave a pleased grin when finally we staggered out of the ranch-house, and I felt a lump in my throat. I gave him a slap on the shoulder in appreciation of the effort he'd put in.

In that moment, despite sundry cuts and bruises, I was the proudest father in the world.

Tommy surprised me some.

'What should we do about the ranch, Pa? Should we fire it?'

He was little, but by God, he was going to be a young firebrand someday!

'No, son, just let's get ourselves home. I don't think we'll hear from Tad Grainger for awhile.'

'But we shouldn't let him get away with all this, Pa.'

'He won't get away with it, believe me, Tommy. I think it's high time we took a visit to Wichita and looked up the Land Records office and did a little digging around, and I've got me a complaint to put to your brother, Ruth. It's time the circuit judge came to town.'

FIVE

But it wasn't as easy as that, and I certainly under-estimated Tad Grainger. And that wasn't the only mistake I made. My only excuse was that I've never been a devious man. I've always considered myself law-abiding and peaceful and tried to be a good neighbour. Now I found that wasn't enough. A feller who needed to defend his family and his land had to fight fire with fire … and it was certainly fire!

Back home, I gave a great spiel about how careful we must all be about moving about the range, and sticking close to home and stressing the youngsters should never go anywhere without permission and having someone with them.

It didn't go down well. Tabby saw the sense of it. She'd had a taste of what it was like to be kidnapped and the fear was still with her. But the boys turned down their mouths and I could see mutiny in their eyes. It was a reflection on their budding manhood. There's no one more foolhardy than a spunky kid whose one idea is to prove himself a man. It gets between him and his brains. I know. I was like that myself at the same age.

But there was one thing doing a man's chores around the place and doing them good, and putting his fool head on the line for a feud of none of his making. I was determined that if either of the boys stepped out of line, I'd come down on them good and proper. They'd never been subjected to my really mean side. I hoped they never would. But the first foolish trick they played, with an idea of helping the situation, they'd be wondering what had hit them. I was so determined to keep them safe.

The rest of the outfit were warned and Mickey O'Rourke gave the boys a chance to leave if they wished. I'm glad to say that none of them took up the offer. It paid to be a good boss.

I gave Ruth a chance to return to town and stay with her brother but she too declined the offer and so we forted up and made a few rules and waited to see what might transpire.

Two days went by, all quiet and I was beginning to think that Tad had had a bellyful and would stay in his own backyard. But I was wrong. He'd taken the time to organize a meeting with some of the dirt farmers and spread his poison to them.

He was a glib bastard if nothing else!

A pity I didn't know of his devious activities until later when I choked the information out of one of the marauding bastards who came on the third night and set the barn ablaze.

It would have been a damn sight worse if I hadn't been lying awake thinking of Ruth sleeping with Tabby instead of me. I was feeling horny and lonely and thinking that the sooner we could make that trip to Wichita the better and maybe get the business at the Land Records Office all done as well as get married. It was all wishful thinking stuff, but it didn't get me settled to sleep.

Then I became conscious of something peculiar, and suddenly it came to me that I could hear cows bawling at intervals, which shouldn't have been so for they always settled at night when the nighthawks were around to hum to them and keep 'em quiet.

Fortunately they were in the home pastures, gathered in to rest the far ranges and allow the scanty grass to recover. We were carrying rather more head than usual and making ready for cutting out those that were destined for the cattle yards.

I got me out of bed. No sense lying wondering what was up. I remembered Mickey was doing nighthawk for the first hours of the night. I'd take a ride and see for myself what was the matter. Maybe we were in for a storm and the restless animals would sense it.

I'd find Mickey and we could have a cigarette together and if the cattle started to move then he'd welcome another pair of hands. It would also take care of the itch in my longjohns!

I found Mickey and he was uneasy.

'What's the matter with them? How long have they been restless?'

'An hour or more. I don't understand it. They were bedded down for the night and when I rode round to the other side, and checked with young Bill and Hornsey, everything was fine and we shared a coffee and had a bite and I rode on right round and there was nothing stirring. Now it looks as if something's spooked them. But there's no hint of a storm, no smell of sulphur, nothing.'

'I'll ride with you. I can't sleep anyway. Might as well do something useful.' We rode slowly, singing quietly and turning back the odd beast who lumbered to his feet and tossed his head ready to start walking, if not running.

There was no warning when the barn went up in flames. I cursed. It all happened at once. Shots were fired from different angles and the herded animals reminded me of a rippling expanse of water in the fitful moonlight as they heaved themselves to their feet ready to run.

I was conscious of Mickey O'Rourke yelling and trying to stop the first charge and pulling his gun and then he disappeared into the slow-moving mass of animals that was fast becoming a stampede.

I backed off. The barn was next to the ranch-house. The herd could go to hell but I had to get to Ruth and my family.

Suddenly all was confusion, noise and choking dust as the hooves of going on for 5,000 head of cattle churned up the ground. Then I found I was in the midst of the moving mass and I felt my mare tremble under me as we were swept along with the now maddened steers.

Gradually I managed to drag the mare's head to one side and as we galloped with the mob, we slowly filtered out of the mainstream, but not without a bad stumble as a charging bull floundered into the mare's flank leaving her limping. I gritted my teeth and literally lifted her until she once more got into her stride.

Then, hardening my heart to the trusty mare's obvious strained hock, I urged her on until we came to the ranch-house and the burning barn, where I found the crew fighting the blaze with buckets of water from the nearby well. I left the mare trembling and blowing her bellows in the shelter of the corral and ran madly to the house but all were outside begrimed and doing what was necessary. Ruth was dishevelled and sooty and pumping water while the boys and the oldsters tossed water on to the sides and roof of the house nearest to the barn.

I saw at once there was no saving the barn and we'd be lucky just to contain the blaze so that sparks did not alight on the now very wet ranch-house roof. But there was still the cookhouse and the blacksmith's shop to watch out for and so for the next three hours there was no time to talk but to get on and subdue the fire.

At the end of all our hard work and struggle we saved the ranch itself, and the blacksmith's shop but the cookhouse and the barn and the crew's bunkhouse were nothing but smoking ruins. I thanked my stars that the wind had blown the way it did, or else nothing would have saved the ranch.

I surveyed the ruins with an arm about Ruth and Tabby. Tabby was all in as was young Tommy. I'd seen them and Billy relaying buckets of water all night and I was mighty proud of them. Ruth, bless her, had rolled her sleeves up and carted out of the house anything she thought precious enough to save if the old wooden house had gone up. She'd also managed to brew coffee for the men on a makeshift campfire well out of the way of the conflagration.

It was while Ruth was tending her fire and

watching the precariously balanced coffeepot that one of Tad Grainger's fire raisers got cocky and snaked in to watch the fun. He saw Ruth, all alone, and rashly took a chance. His arm about her throat prevented her from screaming and big woman though she was, he had her down and was straddling her with a hand up her skirt when I happened along to collect coffee for the boys.

I saw the struggle in the orange glare of the flames some 200 yards away and I ran as I'd never run before and before he realized what was happening, I'd picked him up by the scruff of the neck and I was shaking him like a wild beast shakes its prey. I could have killed him but a wisp of caution stopped me. I wanted information and I was going to get it.

I didn't stop to look if Ruth was all right. I just went to town on the bastard and as it was, I nearly choked the life out of him before I allowed him to speak.

'It was Grainger who sent you, wasn't it?' I panted as the stranger hawked and gagged. He eventually nodded violently as I tightened my grip. I wasn't being particular.

'Who else was with you? Answer me, or I'll tear your tongue out!'

That set him off feebly trying to fight me off and for a few minutes I subjected him to some well-aimed punches not forgetting his attack on

Ruth. The punches to the groin finally broke him and brought tears to his eyes. That was when he told me about Tad Grainger's meeting with the dirt farmers and how small herds of our beef had been siphoned off and quietly turned on to the farmers' land which helped to persuade them to act with him. Tonight's fire-raising had been a unanimous decision by some of the hotheads to drive Drexel out. He was just a paid hand and did what he was told.

I gave him another leathering and explained that that was on behalf of the woman he tried to violate. Then I let him slink off with a message for Grainger ringing in his ears.

'Tell the bastard I'm staying put and I'm coming for him when I'm good and ready and he'd better have his gun oiled and to hand!'

Holding Ruth and Tabby, I surveyed the ruins as the rest of the crew poked amongst the remains for anything to salvage. I cursed hard and my heart was black. I could nearly taste the hate in me. I'd get Tad Grainger even if I had to go to hell to do it.

SIX

My first instinct was to go after Tad Grainger and beat hell out of him. Then I remembered my kids and two oldsters depending on me, and Ruth whom I was quickly becoming dependent on for comforts of home which I'd never really had ... the decent grub, the bright and shining house, fresh-smelling clothes and Tabby who was fast turning from a ragamuffin into a better behaved little girl.

I couldn't risk all that by a dumb act which might bring all the townsfolk down on our heads. I had to act cautious. I had to remember that feeling was running high about Billy and his supposed backshooting of poor old Jesse.

Folks were mighty peculiar especially in a mob. It only took a man with a gift of the gab to sway the rabble in any way he wished, and Tad Grainger was a good talker.

So I took time to think and plan and with Ruth's help we got ourselves organized, and she even rearranged the sleeping quarters so that the men could bunk down temporary-like in the ranch itself. It was a tight fit but we managed.

Grub was the big problem. All our stores were kept in a cellar half underground for coolness which had been dug next to the cookhouse. All the root vegetables were ruined and the spare sacks of flour and other dry goods. We only had what Ruth had brought into the house for convenience so a trip to town was necessary.

I had a feeling that Grainger and his lickarses would be waiting for our next move which would mean a trip into Sweetwater. Well, if he was waiting to backshoot us on the trail, he was disappointed because we cut over rough ground and the old wagon got a pasting but we drove into Wichita, Tommy and me, armed with a list as long as your arm from Ruth. I left Billy in the store ticking the items off his list and I took me along to the Land Records Office and sure enough, old Jesse had turned the ranch over to Tad Grainger and not in the very far past either.

The date made me think more than ever that Tad had engineered old Jesse's death. He might not have fired the shot but the fact remained, Jesse's death was a Godsend especially as he was for getting leg-shackled to the preacher's daughter.

I had a gut feeling. I was sure I was right. It was because of the girl that Tad Grainger had gone bad.

I took the opportunity to go find me a drink and listen to the talk in the best saloon in town, The Golden Garter. It was a place I knew well. You could rely on good rye and the beer didn't give you the trots.

Some of the ranchers were in town and the talk got round to rustling and I kept myself quiet and listened and found out that I wasn't the only one whose cattle had been driven off in the past.

I'd wondered at the slick way Grainger's men had torn down my fences and driven my cattle on to the dirt farmers' land. Maybe Grainger was quietly adding to Jesse's herd the quick way. It had occurred to me several times that Jesse's cows were multiplying fast. It also occurred to me that maybe Jesse hadn't known what was going on, that when he'd found out … That was another reason for wanting old Jesse dead.

Tad Grainger, murderer of his benefactor, rustler and now fire-raiser. Yes, the cap fitted well.

Then I pricked up my ears when I heard a little feller with a big walrus moustache speak up for the first time.

'I knew Jesse Coates when he first took up his

ranch when I was a shaver. He had a sister in those days. Came to visit once with a new husband. Forget his name, but he was some dude from back East. Nice feller but quiet. Didn't know a horse-apple from a bull's pizzle. I think they went to Chicago or some such.'

He stopped when all those listening stared at him.

'How come you know so much?' a big man with silver conches on a wide black stetson asked.

'I worked for Jesse as a wrangler. That was before I married Agnes and worked for her pa on our ranch.'

'I thought Jesse had no kin. Tad Grainger always made out he had no one. Mind you, Tad was always a fly bastard. I wouldn't be surprised if he didn't target Jesse from the very beginning. He was supposed to be a cattle buyer from Chicago when he came to Sweetwater Springs. I wouldn't trust him as far as I could kick him!'

'He runs a tight outfit and there's some hardcases amongst them.'

'And he's got more men on his payroll than he lets on. There's a crew living rough in a line camp out in the hills. Now why should he do that?' another rancher chimed in. 'We meet up with them sometimes when we're hunting strays and they're not a friendly bunch. Always hardware at the ready.'

'You think they're mixed up with the rustling, Chuck?' the first man asked.

The little man looked both ways and lowered his head.

'Keep your voice down, Socko. I always have a funny feeling one of these strangers could be one of Grainger's men.' He looked hard at me and I stared right back. He wasn't scaring me none. I had a twitch in my trigger finger and a single movement would put him in his place.

'You wanting to make a point, mister?'

'Nope!' I replied and stood my ground. 'I ain't here to talk but drink. Is there a law against it?'

'Not if that's all you're doing. Do you know Tad Grainger?'

'Yep.'

'So! You're one of his men!'

'Nope!'

'Then how do you know him?' Now everyone listening stopped drinking to listen. Everything had gone quiet.

'Unfortunately I'm a neighbour of his. I'm Drexel of the DXL ranch and his men fired my ranch. Fortunately we saved the ranch itself but half of my buildings have gone and I'm in a rare mean mood.'

'And why did he do that?'

'Because the bastard wants me off my place. Wants to expand Jesse Coates's ranch.'

A man listening nodded.

'He's speaking the truth, Socko. I saw smoke from way over his part of the range a few nights ago. I thought it was a bush fire and wondered whether Grainger was in trouble.'

Tension went out of those listening and I finished my drink and as the talk turned to other things I took my leave. But the snippet of information about Jesse having a sister stayed with me. Why hadn't the old man ever mentioned her?

Later, I collared the little feller and asked him about Jesse but he hadn't much more information to tell. But he did know that the sister's name was Jane and her husband was a clerk in a meat-packing factory.

I was very thoughtful when I went to seek out Tommy.

He'd done good and I rewarded him with a new leather waistcoat and a good steak dinner at Lin Hoo's eatery. Then we picked out new boots for Billy and the oldsters and some ribbons and stuff to make garments for Tabby and a bottle of scent and I personally chose a hat with a feather for Ruth and a pair of fine kid gloves and I looked twice at a flounced gown in a bright blue but I couldn't see Ruth wearing it. It was more for the likes of Alice Symons. So I settled for a parasol and another bottle of scent. All womenfolk liked to smell nice.

Ruth was more pleased with the list of goods

than the presents we'd brought back. At least she didn't show much pleasure to me but later, Tabby told me Ruth had confessed to never having real luxury things and though she wouldn't have much use for the hat and parasol and gloves, she'd treasure them always.

Maybe I should have settled on a few bolts of cloth and let them work out what they wanted to do with 'em. I'd know better next time. Hopefully we'd go to Wichita together and she could buy what she wanted and we would get spliced and all this agonizing waiting would be over.

The punchers worked with a will and soon got the framework for a new bunkhouse up. We were lucky. One of the crew had worked as a lumberjack way up in Montana and I got him to make the new bunkhouse bigger and design a better eating area. We salvaged the old iron stove and built a wall and chimneybreast tough enough to stand any onslaught. Down below was a new cellar and when the sawn timber was added on to the walls, the bunkhouse became a small fort.

I was pleased. I had this gut feeling that from now on we needed reinforced buildings. The punchers were full of enthusiasm and any good ideas from any of them were taken up and used. After all, they were building their own place.

We were a happy bunch and gradually due to the success of the new building, we let our guard slip. It was my fault. I should have known better.

I was with the timber hauling team and we'd sawn down six straight trees and dressed them ready for the haul back to the ranch. We'd had trouble with the horses. There were eight strong draft horses. Six were experienced and two were newcomers owing to the fact that two of the others were laid off because of leg injuries. They didn't mix well and we'd had trouble.

But now we'd got the heavy long logs chained together and ready for the long pull, and it was as the men struggled with the team that the shots came. Hank, the oldest of the men, gave a yell and spun round and fell nearly under a plunging horse's hooves.

I cursed and dragged him free and already two of the men were firing into a stand of trees. I shouted to the man holding the leading horses to hang on and hold 'em, but be sure to keep them between himself and the bastards who were attacking us.

Then I dived for cover and as sporadic fire came from the stand of trees I thought it would be a smart move to belly around and to the back of those targeting us.

It took time and I heard a few yelps as our crew settled down to do some fancy shooting.

Then as I worked my way around I saw that someone else had the same idea. I couldn't believe my eyes and something icy froze the pit of my stomach. It was Tommy. Then the ice turned to fire and fury hit me. What in hell was Tommy doing here?

I'm afraid I lost control and moved through the brush like a maddened bull. He heard me crashing through the undergrowth and twisting about lay looking at me flat on his back. His face paled. Tommy's face always seemed to shrivel when he was in bad trouble. His skin took on a translucent waxy glow and his eyes seemed too big for his face. But he was right to be frightened. I could have killed him.

'What in God's name are you doing here?' I didn't wait for his answer but let rip with some choice oaths and a colourful description of the kind of fool he was. He started to cry.

'Hell! If you're so goddamn keen to grow up, stop that snivelling!' I barked gruffly.

He wiped his nose on his sleeve.

'Ruth sent me,' he managed to stutter and I imagined he had a great big gob-stopper sticking in his throat. 'She said to tell you that riders were coming up the valley ....'

'And they got here, by the looks of things!' I answered savagely. Then I caught his eye and saw how I had wounded him. 'I'm sorry son, I shot my mouth off without thought, but I was concerned for you.' I pulled him roughly to me and gave his thin body a hug and then as the shots were coming faster, I put him from me. 'You keep out of trouble, you hear me? And whatever you see, don't try to interfere, so lie low, boy.'

'What you going to do, Pa?' There was a tremble in his voice he couldn't control. It made his voice squeak.

'I'm aiming to get behind these bastards and give 'em a surprise.'

'Ruth made me bring the old shotgun. It's way back over there.' He pointed behind him.

For the first time I smiled. My rifle was propped up beside that load of logs and I only had one gun strapped to my side.

'Good boy, Tommy. I'll collect it and the first shot will be for you!'

I snaked away and duly found the gun and then I ran bunched down nearly double until I came within sight of three spaced out gunmen with their arses for targets. I couldn't miss. It was a matter of which one to choose. It would be like shooting sitting ducks. I took aim at the widest, fattest arse.

'I wouldn't do that if I were you.' I heard the click of a trigger somewhere behind me. I cursed and obeyed when he told me to drop the shotgun. Then, holding my hands above my head, I half turned to look at the man who'd got the drop, making sure my handgun was hidden by my body.

He was a big man with long blond shaggy hair and bristles on his chin which reminded me of a pig's. He was wise to the trick I was trying to pull. He laughed.

'Take off the belt and drop it at your feet.' The friendly smile disappeared and his face twisted in a grimace. 'I understand you're a wily bastard by Tad Grainger's reckoning.'

'So, you're one of his hired killers, eh? What did he tell you?'

'That you're treading on his corns and he wants you out and I'm going to see that you go. The others? I don't care whether they live or die. Punchers are two to the dollar, but you … I've got my orders to see that you go without any hassle.'

'And how do you mean to do that?'

'Easy. You have a daughter, Tabby?'

'Yeh, I've got a daughter ....' Then it hit me. 'You bastard, you've got her, haven't you?'

The man nodded, an amused grin on his face. 'Yes, and your son, Billy. A pity he didn't come quietly. I think his ribs got hurt. He's mighty fond of his sister.'

I ground my teeth. After all I'd told them, the young fools had strayed from the ranch. The low deep growl of the man brought me alert.

'We left the old men and the woman. She fought like a wild cat until the Mex pinned her hand to the wall with his knife. She'd caught him a wallop with a yard broom and he got mad. It was her own fault. Women should stay out of these things.'

I nodded, brains working fast but not producing any plan of action. I felt paralysed.

'So where are you taking Billy and Tabby?'

'Up in the hills. That's the boss's idea, until we get sorted out about this here ranch. Grainger will do anything to get it, believe me.'

'I suppose they're on their way to that back-of-beyond line cabin of Grainger's?'

I spoke carelessly with my head down. I was considering the chances of diving for a small boulder about four feet from where I was standing. It looked loose enough to heave up and throw, but how fast was this mountain of a man, or more to the point, how fast were his reflexes?

There was only one way to find out and I gazed past his shoulder and I twitched my lips and the fool fell for it and swivelled about to see if he was being stalked. That was enough for me to fling myself forward and heave up the rock high above my head and as he turned to me again, I brought it down on his head with all the force I could muster. It hit his forehead fair and square and I heard bone crunch and he went down like a pole-axed steer.

I scarcely glanced at him after I saw the state of his skull. He wouldn't be gunning for anyone on this side of hell ever again.

I grabbed his guns and rifle and stepped nearer the crouching gunmen who'd been kept busy blazing away at my punchers, oblivious as to what had been going on behind them.

I shot one in the arse and saw a spreading red stain spoil his pants and I knew his piles would never trouble him again.

It was tricky when the other two both turned and let off snap shots in my direction. I got one, and one of the punchers got the other as the man panicked and stood up in full view.

I was turning away when a fourth man I never reckoned on, blundered out of the bushes and took aim at me. I saw him and ducked as he tossed off a shot but suddenly he flung up his arms and seemed to leap back before he fell heavily amongst the stones with blood pouring from several wounds. I stood, surprised and then Tommy appeared from behind a boulder and he was retching and throwing his last two meals all over the landscape.

I saw he'd got Uncle Jed's old sawn-off shotgun he used for duckshooting. Ruth had sure made certain we would have extra guns up here which was just as well. I wondered how I'd missed that when I'd got the other.

But the kid had done well. I strode over to him and held him while he finished cleaning out his stomach, then he looked up at me all pale and sorrowful-like.

'Pa, promise me you won't tell Billy or Grandpa or Uncle Jed about me being sick?'

I kept a straight face. I knew how I felt the first time I killed a man and I was a lot older than he was.

'I swear it, Tommy and I want you to know you saved my life.'

I think it was at that time me and Tommy got a new understanding of each other. From that time on, I never regarded him as a kid no more. A pity maybe, by some folk's standards but by the laws of survival he was becoming a fully fledged man.

Then my mind flashed back to Billy and Tabby and what was the situation back at the ranch. We both hurried over to the rest of the men and found two hurt but not badly and we left the logs and untangled the frightened horses, freeing them to follow us back to the corral.

We rode like the wind and galloped into the yard as if the Devil himself was after us. I swung myself off my horse leaving him to someone else to corral and feed and I ran indoors and found Pa and Uncle Jed looking after Ruth who was tucked up under a quilt on the settle in the inglenook by the stove. She had a rough bandage swathed about her hand and wrist.

'How is she?' I barked at the two men.

'Shush! you clumsy fool,' Pa hissed, 'she's asleeping. Got a nasty wound through the palm of her hand.'

'I'll kill the bastard that did it when I catch up with him,' I raved in as near as a whisper as I could get.

'It was a greaser that did it. Young, with oily black hair and a moustache that went all around his mouth.'

I knelt down beside her studying her unconscious features. She lay, pale and drawn and there was a small frown between her eyes. I was aware of how dear she had become to me. I no longer thought her plain, her wide generous mouth and her eyes are the things I saw and remembered.

Those beautiful eyes fluttered open and widened as she saw me leaning over her. I'm only a plain clumsy feller, but in that moment I swear something wonderful happened between us, something I never really knew existed. She put an arm up and encircled my neck and I gently raised her so that I could cuddle her and I had the feeling that all was known between us. We were as one, and I confess it, I cried.

It finished up her comforting me instead of the other way round.

The whole incident altered my way of thinking about her. I was no longer in awe of her, or awkward about anything. It was as if she was the better part of myself.

It also left me with a great anger that would

have to be resolved. There was to be no more pussyfooting around.

Tad Grainger might hassle me and get away with it, but now Ruth had been hurt and two of my kids taken. It was time for all out war.

Reluctantly I put her from me.

'I can't stay, love. I've got to go after them.'

She clung to me, vulnerable and weak.

'Hal, you'll be careful? I'm not one for saying much, but …' and then it came out in a rush, 'I love you, you know.'

I nodded, a nasty sore lump in my throat.

'And me, likewise,' I managed to croak and then tore myself away. At the door I paused and looked back and she was watching me all anxious-like. 'Pa and Uncle Jed will watch out for you. I'll be back, don't fret.' And then I was running down the veranda steps to Tommy who was holding a fresh horse.

Once aboard, he thrust a clumsy packet of grub into my hand.

'Bread and meat, Pa. Shove it into your saddle-bag.' Then he hesitated. 'Can I come with you?' But he knew the answer and for once he was being sensible.

'No, son. You stay around and help the oldsters. I'm taking Mickey and most of the boys who can handle a rifle good. There's got to be someone in charge and you're it!'

He nodded and I think he was proud to be trusted to be in charge. Mickey had chosen six of the most seasoned riders and soon we were on our way.

It was time to take the war into the enemy camp.

SEVEN

We made good time considering the rough terrain we travelled over. The risk was to the horses' legs. We'd cut across country towards Grainger's ranch, but now we hit the dirt-track and road once again. I was still boiling inside and ready to take risks. Mickey, by my side during the whole of the mad gallop, now glanced my way and said gruffly, 'We should stop and have a confab as to what we should do next. You know Grainger runs a hard outfit and they'll be expecting us.'

I considered his words and slowed down, partly to think and partly to ease the horses. The road led upwards and wound round a tall needle of red rock and then plunged down the other side ... a good place for an ambush, if it was Grainger's idea of luring me into the open by snatching Tabby.

So we walked our horses with rifles cocked and laid across pommels and our eyes every whichway. The men behind us automatically spread out showing how all our minds ran on the same lines.

So it was a shock when we turned the corner and looked down into that small divide and saw the overturned buggy with wheels still spinning and a horse down on its side and another struggling to free itself. More sinister, however, was the small crumpled body of a woman lying dangerously close to the surviving horse.

I swore. I could see the skid marks of wheels careering down the winding bank and as we set off at a steady trot, we passed the place where the left wheel had hit a boulder and the horses had taken off in fright.

Mickey O'Rourke was the first to reach her. I concentrated on cutting the harness of the remaining horse. I saw briefly that the other animal had taken the brunt of the accident and it had a broken neck.

I tethered the remaining horse which was shaking and sweating and soothed it until it quieted, so I missed the sight of Mickey actually bringing the female round. There were plenty of helpers, however, as all the men crowded around to look at the pretty girl in blue with her honey-blonde hair tumbling about her shoulders.

It wasn't often the men had the chance of seeing a woman in disarray, especially a good woman, and they were acting like dogs after a bitch on heat!

Then Mickey surprised me. He grinned at me.

'I think we've got the answer, boss. Meet Miss Charlotte Pierce.'

I looked at him questioningly. He raised his eyebrows and glanced down at the young lady who was now sitting up but with her head down. She'd just had a swig of Mickey's rotgut which he carried for emergencies and was struggling with the after effects.

Suddenly a great light dawned. This was the girl Tad Grainger was sparking. I saw Mickey's drift. We had a bargaining tool ....

I knelt down beside the girl.

'Miss Pierce ... ma'am?'

She lifted a heavy head. I could see the bruise on her forehead and the slight cut that bled a little. She'd taken a nasty toss and fallen hard. Her delicate body would be stiff and sore for a few days to come.

'Yes?'

'What happened? What made the horses run downbank?'

'There was a big bird, I think it was an eagle and it was swooping down on an animal when we turned the corner. I think it was a jackrabbit and it was struggling as the bird took off. I screamed at it and waved my whip, and it dropped the rabbit which started to run. The bird came down in front of the horses and they reared up and then bolted. I pulled on the brake which made the buggy veer from side to side. Then it hit something hard. I couldn't hold the horses even though I applied the brake. I've never been so frightened in my life.'

'Then that dead horse put a foot in a hole,' I indicated the dead animal. 'It's got a broken fetlock as well as a broken neck and the buggy went over. You're lucky you're alive! Are you well enough to ride, Miss Pierce?'

Mickey glared at me. 'That's a fool question, boss. I'll carry her in front of me.'

I shrugged. I could see Mickey was taken with her. The other fellers looked at one another and stood back. No one messed with Mickey when there was something he wanted.

So we rode up to Grainger's place with Miss Pierce well to the fore, which was a good thing. We might have been greeted with a hail of bullets.

Grainger stepped out onto his veranda with a rifle in his hand as soon as we rode up. I saw his face redden as he recognized Miss Pierce.

'Charlotte! I've been worrying and wondering why you hadn't got here.'

'But you didn't come looking for me, Tad. If you wanted me here for some reason I should have thought you would have come yourself, not have one of your punchers put a note under my door during the night! Why the secrecy, Tad?' Her voice was cold.

I was surprised. By Tad's account in the saloons, she was as good as promised to him. Had it been wishful thinking?

'Yes, well, I can explain all that when you come inside.' Grainger glared at us all. It was a sticky moment. 'How come you're with this trash?'

I felt the ripple of resentment run through my boys, and there was a concerted movement of rifle butts.

'They're not trash, Tad!'

'Well, whatever they are, how come you're with them?'

'I had an accident, Tad, and they rescued me. Haven't you noticed there's no buggy?'

Tad Grainger swallowed. I smiled to myself. I could imagine Tad's brains working overtime on how to deal with this situation. It was time I showed this girl just what a bastard he was.

'I've come for Tabby and Billy, Grainger. You're coming for a ride with us. We know they're being held in that line cabin of yours. Trouble is, that place is like a fort and you can save a lot of bloodshed. We'll leave what you did to Ruth on the books. We can deal with that later.'

Miss Pierce looked from Tad to me.

'What did he do to Ruth? You *are* talking about

Mrs Lowrie?'

'Ask him, and while you're at it, ask him about the two old men he beat up!'

'Tad, what's going on? What's all this about Ruth and Tabby and Billy?'

'Come inside and I'll tell you.'

'Do you seriously believe we'll let Miss Pierce go, Grainger? If you do, you're loco. She's coming with us to ensure no tricks. Is that clear?'

'But .....!' The girl swivelled round to look at Mickey. 'I can't possibly ride any farther!'

'Boss, maybe we should give Miss Pierce time to eat something and freshen up and a cup of coffee wouldn't come amiss for us all.' He glanced round at the riders.

I saw the sense to that. No need to deprive us all of sustenance. After all, we'd ridden nigh on three hours and it had been a long time since breakfast.

'Right! Dismount fellers, and you, Mickey, watch Miss Pierce and I'll watch this slippery bastard. The first move from one of your men, Grainger, and you'll get a slug in the belly.'

Grainger was alone in the homestead. I wondered why and I thought of him sending a message for her to come to him, rather than he go and visit her.

The men took advantage of coffee brewing on the stove. Mickey saw Miss Pierce was fed much to the anger of Tad Grainger who had to sit under my watchful eye and a gun pointing up his nose.

We ate our own rations and Mickey escorted the young lady to the privy and back much to her embarrassment, but it had to be done as we weren't sure how she regarded the ranch boss.

Then began the long ride to the very northern edge of the J Bar C ranch and the farther we rode the madder I got. I could imagine the ordeal it must have been for Billy what with his bad ribs and all, not forgetting young Tabby and her not used to long horseback riding. They'd both be tuckered out.

Grainger rode alongside me, head down and silent but I sensed an alertness about him that made me uneasy. I watched him like a hawk while Mickey O'Rourke rode behind with Miss Pierce, and by the sounds coming from behind it was mighty like Mickey was on some kind of Sunday outing. I hoped the love-struck fool was keeping his wits about him, as were the other riders strung out behind him.

I tried needling Grainger to get some response, but he was a hard nut to crack, his face a granite mask as he gave me a quick glance.

'No good, Drexel. I don't aim to rise to your bait! Miss Pierce has an understanding with me. I want what I wants and she gets what she wants. Savvy?'

'And you think you'll still get what you want?'

'Yes, why not? Me? I've got patience. If you wait long enough and work at it, then you always come out tops.'

Why are you so sure this time?'

He laughed. 'If I told you that, then you'd know as much as me.'

'Why were you waiting for Miss Pierce … alone, with no back-up?'

'Because I figured it was settling-up time. I want that place of yours. Drexel, and I'm willing to pay you out right and proper, even now ….'

'You aren't in a position to bargain, Grainger,' I snarled. 'Just as you're in no position to bargain with Miss Pierce, because I think that was what you were proposing to do?'

'What goes on between me and Charlotte is none of your affair!'

'By the look of her and my foreman together, I think it has become my affair! They're getting on very well as you can see!'

Grainger gritted his teeth. 'It doesn't matter what she thinks about O'Rourke. It's about what she's willing to do to save her pa!'

'Her pa? What in hell's name as he got to do with anything?'

Grainger shrugged and looked ahead with that stony glare that I thought made the man loco. That was it. He was nuts. Too much patience, a mighty lot of frustration and delusions of his own importance had finally taken him over the edge and he was all that much more dangerous because he appeared to the ordinary observer as just another arrogant rancher who liked his own way.

I saw by the frozen look on the girl's face that Mickey O'Rourke's earlier blarney had been for a reason. I breathed a sigh of relief. I couldn't have believed that Mickey would be bowled over by a woman so quickly, not at his time of life, but had used his gift of the gab to release the stress in her. Maybe he had meant some of the things he'd told her, but now I guessed he'd taken time to bring her up to date on what had been happening and she'd come to some conclusions of her own.

She carefully avoided looking at Grainger. I guessed something would blow when we reached that line cabin.

Something did blow, but it wasn't Miss Pierce. It came from an entirely different quarter.

We drew up at the top of a small valley covered in grass. It was a good vista with rich herbage and some cattle grazing quietly in the shade of some trees. There was a narrow stream running through the bottom end of the valley and I knew any cattleman would give plenty for this sight. A pity it hadn't been in the centre of Jesse Coates's land for there would never have been any hassle between him and us Drexels. Not that by the look of it there would have been enough water for all the stock held on Coates land. Still, water is water and there might be a good spring.

However, that was by the way. Now I could see why the line cabin was built where it was. A crew could stay out in these wilds for weeks on end, and I got the funny feeling that this place wasn't just an innocent cabin for a crew to lay up while fencing or branding calves or some suchlike. No, this was more of an outlaw's lair.

We cantered down towards the cabin and now saw that there were several other buildings not noticeable because they were built in the shadow of a stand of trees. There was a giant watchtower and beside it a large watertank and I concluded that in the dry season the small stream dried up.

Grainger was sitting more upright now and he looked more cheerful and I wondered why.

'What in hell's got into you?' I growled and cocked my rifle and I heard several rifles click behind me.

Grainger grinned at me.

'Look up there and you'll see why!'

I looked up at the watchtower and my blood ran cold. One of Grainger's riders was pointing a rifle but that wasn't what put a snake hissing up and down my back, it was the fact that a man was hanging by his wrists on the outside of the tower.

Then came the unmistakable sounds of several high-powered rifles being cocked and I looked around sharply and Grainger's men came out of hiding. I should have guessed it.

Quick as a flash I leaned over and heaving, dragged Grainger from his horse and we both fell to the ground in a welter of thrashing legs and then Mickey O'Rourke was down beside us and we dragged Grainger to his feet and I drew my gun and poked it into his ear.

'Draw your watchdogs off, Grainger or I'll blow you to hell,' I growled and shoved the gun viciously so that he was in danger of losing his head.

His men stood watchful but relaxed when he waved a hand to back off.

'Now, Grainger, I want those kids of mine. Tell that jackal of yours to bring 'em out pronto, wherever they are and do it now and while we're getting things straightened out, tell that bastard up there to haul the old man in and loosen his ropes. Now!' I jerked Grainger's arms behind his back until he yelped.

'Ned,' he bawled, 'pull the reverend in and cut his wrists free and let him climb down the ladder. There, does that please you Drexel?'

'Yeh, but not half as much as when I see my kids. Get 'em out here, Grainger, or else I'm going to forget I'm a white man and try a few Indian tricks on you!'

He thought I was blustering. He laughed.

'They're my ace in the hole, Drexel. Nobody knows where they are, only me. Kill me and they die!'

By God, he sounded like he was telling the truth!

'So it's a Mexican stand-off, you think, Grainger?'

Grainger grinned and nodded. 'You get what you want when I get what I want! That's fair isn't it?'

'You want Miss Pierce?'

'Charlotte? Oh no, I want something much more important than Charlotte. There's other women, you know. You know what I want, Drexel. I'll trade your kids for the right to buy your land. I'll pay fair and square and you can start again somewhere else. I'm being reasonable, man ....'

I clipped him under the chin. He sprawled in the dirt and I dragged him up and I planted a couple of stingers, that would hurt but not do any real damage.

'Where you hiding those kids?' I panted and raised a fist to flatten his nose. He lunged to one side and I missed. He laughed wildly.

'You'll never find 'em, Drexel, not until the rains come anyway and that will be too late! I've got you against a wall and a hard place, Drexel, so why not give in and negotiate like a wise man and put those kids out of their misery?'

That was when I shot away his left knee-cap.

I was aware of confusion behind me, of cocking

rifles and a woman's screams and then a couple of shots as a stooped figure staggered at a run from the bottom of the watchtower.

I was too busy holding the thrashing body of Grainger and trying to choke the whereabouts of Tabby and Billy out of him to anticipate what was to happen next.

All I knew was when was two bony hands pulled me roughly aside so that I sprawled headlong and my gun was snatched and then I was deafened by a blast that seemed to engulf me. Stunned, I looked up at the Reverend Pierce holding my smoking Colt and tears were streaming down his cheeks.

I looked from him to Grainger and there was a hole the size of two fists seeping a flood of crimson in his chest. I swore.

'You stupid old bugger! You killed him before I found out where my kids are!'

He wasn't listening. He dropped to his knees and started to pray, shoulders shaking and I vaguely saw Charlotte go to him and put an arm about him.

For me, I was in a turmoil and if Mickey O'Rourke hadn't taken charge I would have been a sitting duck. As it was, Grainger's men were smart enough to realize that all this ducking and diving was none of their business and like all professional killers, made a clean break.

They were bunched together ready to ride back to the J Bar C to collect their gear before riding out to find other jobs.

'Any of you jaspers know where the kids are?' I grated. 'A hundred bucks is riding on your answer.'

I saw the men look at each other and then the one whom I took to be their leader inched his mount forward.

'Mister, we didn't know there were kids involved. There was only one man who did Grainger's dirty work, he and his big pard, Trantor, and some of the boys went on a special mission and never come back.'

'The man you talk about was he a Mex?'

'Yeh, a slimy little bastard who was always playing with a knife. Keeps it in a pouch between his shoulder-blades. Got this habit of raising his hands above his head when cornered and then turns the tables by flashing a knife and believe me, that knife goes where it's aimed!'

I nodded.

'So the Mex took the kids while his big pal came to settle our hash and they're the ones who snuffed it.' I turned to Mickey O'Rourke. 'So now we're looking for a killer Mex who's the only one who knows where those kids are. You any ideas, any of you?' I looked around the bunched riders. 'Any place comes to mind where you could stash two prisoners?'

All their faces were blank and so we let them ride out and I can never describe the utter helplessness and despair I felt for my kids.

It brought out all the meanness in me.

I watched Charlotte help the old man to his feet and support him. He was badly marked about the face as if he'd put up a fight before he was taken.

'You hear anything about my kids while they held you?' I asked more to say something rather than get a real answer.

The old man shook his head. 'They only spoke of Grainger being a fool, and risking his neck for my daughter. That bunch were cattle thieves. You know that, don't you?'

'I guessed. So why did they take you?'

'Because I was called to a dying man. He was a dirt farmer from down the valley and had been shot. He'd seen some cattle with the Drexel brand herded on to his land and he'd gone to give the punchers a piece of his mind. He recognized them as Grainger's men and was shot down. His son found him and called me to him. I told Grainger what I knew and that I forbade him my house and that Charlotte would see him no more.'

'And because Grainger had to have his own way, he had you snatched.'

'And it was on his orders that I was hung outside that watchtower ....'

Suddenly it was as if the realization of what had

happened to him, really hit him. He looked at Charlotte. 'My dear ....'

Then he collapsed in her arms nearly bringing her down with him. Mickey O'Rourke sprang forward and caught him and gently laid him on the ground.

Mickey knelt beside him and then looked up at Charlotte.

'It's not a heart attack. He's fainted with exhaustion.'

I thought he was a very lucky old man.

I left Mickey and Charlotte to do the necessary and I got the boys organized. It was going to be a matter of plain slog and every inch of this land for miles around would have to be searched, every cave, and mound, under every boulder, even in hollow trees would have to be searched and every moment counted.

I put myself in Grainger's place. Where would be the natural hiding-place? I also wondered what had happened to the Mex. Maybe he was guarding those kids ....'

We searched all day in all directions and at nightfall, the boys trickled in, spent and weary, their horses heads drooping after so many miles over rough country.

Charlotte, bless her, had used the outlaws' provisions and rustled up a meal. The smell of beans and onions and stewed beef greeted us and she'd even made a batch of panbread to go with it. We were grateful as our bellies thought our throats were cut.

I lay awake all night amid the snores of the boys who slept on the floor of the cabin with saddles for pillows as Charlotte had the only extra room which was really a store-room. But it wasn't the snores that kept me awake. I was sure enough used to men snoring. It was because of my kids. I could see Tabby's face in the dark, shining at me, tears running down her cheeks. Billy's face came and went, brave and manly and I realized once again just how much these kids meant to me. I'd kill that bastard Mex, if it took the rest of my life to catch up with him. I thought of Ruth, too, and the hurt she'd suffered and I had to get up and go outside and stamp up and down to vent my rage.

Then that frustrating rage cooling a little, I began to think and let my brains take over. What had Grainger said when I asked him one last time where he was holding them?

He'd laughed but what had he said?

I racked my brains, saying the question over and over again and remembering the response. He'd been mighty certain we wouldn't find them … I began to panic and cursed mightily.

Then, like a whisper in my ear, I remembered something. It was his voice as if from far away. 'You'll never find 'em, Drexel, not until the rains come anyway ....'

The rains!

That meant somewhere beside the stream, the only water in the valley, somewhere that was dried up during the dry season as of now.

I gave a great yell, and Mickey O'Rourke stumbled out of the cabin waving his Colt, a confused look in his eyes.

'What is it? Are we being attacked?'

I told him what Grainger had said and without saying a word, went and kicked all the boys awake. The fire in the stove was fanned into flame and soon coffee was brewing and we breakfasted on cold meat and bread.

We were just ready to depart and the first light of day was streaking over the distant hills when Charlotte came out of her little room rubbing her eyes and yawning. Startled, her eyes went to Mickey O'Rourke. I smiled to myself. I don't think that young lady would grieve very much for Tad Grainger.

'You should have called me sooner. I would have made your breakfast.'

'No sweat, ma'am. We're used to doing for ourselves.' He grinned down at her.

'You'll take care?' She raised her pretty eyes to his and I swear she blushed a little.

'I'll take no chances, ma'am,' he answered solemnly. 'There's plenty of us to go catch one slippery Mex. You just keep your mind on your pa, ma'am, and the time will soon pass.'

'My name's Charlotte.' Now she looked panicky as if Mickey might take exception and think her forward. She didn't know Mickey!

'My ma called me Michael but I always get Mickey,' he grinned down at her and mentally I began to plan where they should build their log cabin. I could see when all this was over there was going to be a need for a parson.

I coughed and they both turned to me as if I'd been forgotten.

'Time to ride,' I said succinctly and walked out of the cabin so they could have a last moment of privacy. I'm a soft old fool at heart!

But my mind wasn't really on lovers. I was thinking of those kids spending another night imprisoned and frightened. I wasn't even sure if there were others who knew where they were and waiting for the next move.

We started at the nearest point of the stream searching both banks and up and down stream. There were no signs of horses' tracks so the boys fanned out and Mickey and me picked our way further upstream. We searched around all the big boulders, the stretches of thick brush and any dried up tributary that joined the upper reaches of the stream.

We were losing hope when we came to the

waterfall. It was a puny effort, just a thin trickle of water falling over a lip of slimy rock but I could see when the rains came it would be quite impressive for that place.

I studied it, leaning on the pommel of my saddle as my mare drank at the stream. I could see where the mark would lift the water during the wet season. There was a great hollowed basin where over thousands of years that water had grooved out a passage.

'Let's take a closer look,' I said tersely, and dismounting, ground-hobbled the mare beside a luxuriant clump of green grass. Mickey did likewise.

I doused my head in the clear water. It was cold as if it held meltwater from the far hills. I drank and it was good. Then walking a-ways, we found the jagged cliff was the beginning of a small canyon that stretched way back into the hills. We followed the line of the stream and came at last to the very birthplace of that water.

It was a jumble of rocks, with a mighty great split in the middle, dark and dank as if at some time there had been a great earthquake and underground water had gushed up like a geyser and then carved a passage through the rocks to tumble and eddy into a spring that now obviously attracted a variety of wild animals.

But something about this place didn't seem

right.

'What do you think, Mickey?'

Mickey scratched his head.

'There's something odd. It's like as if it wasn't quite natural. It's as if something's been rearranged. Maybe I'm going loco but don't some of those rocks look as if they've been moved?'

I slapped my leg.

'Damn me for a fool! That's it! Look, over there, wouldn't you say that dirty big rock looks kind of loose! It hasn't got the lichen growing on it and isn't wedged with soil or stones. It looks as if it had been moved fairly recently. Come on, let's have a closer look.'

Mickey climbed higher and looked at it from above.

'Somebody's been here, boss. There's scuff marks and the ground's all churned up. I think we could move this rock quite easily. It'll roll.'

I scrambled up beside him, my heart beating fast. Maybe, just maybe we'd found Grainger's foolproof hiding-place.

It took some effort but not more than two men could manage and with a creak and a groan, the boulder rolled, far enough for a man to slip inside.

Behind it was a natural cave fashioned during the upheaval of the rocks. The walls ran wet as if the actual water gushed up from below farther back. That water could be seeping from the hills. I knew all about water finding its own level and meandering for miles.

I struck a match and looked upwards and saw the signs of water reaching nearly to the roof. That spring would become a torrent when the rains came.

I could hear Mickey breathing heavily behind me. He didn't like enclosed spaces and I knew it was loyalty that kept him with me.

'Anybody there?' I yelled and the words echoed so I knew the cave was a split that went back. 'Billy? Tabby? If you can hear me, shout!'

But all I heard was my own voice.

'Maybe we're on to a loser, boss.' Mickey's voice came uneasily. 'Maybe we should go back.'

His words stiffened my resolve.

'I'm going on. You go back and watch the entrance. I've got my hip flask. Give me your bandana and I'll fold it tight with mine and soak 'em in rotgut and make a torch. I'm going as far back as is possible. I can always feel my way out.'

'But what if there are holes?'

'Use your head, Mickey. This split in the rock was carved out by water and it's smooth underfoot. I'll go as far as I can without light and then when I get as far as I can I'll light up and look around.'

'Maybe we should stick together ....' He didn't sound enthusiastic.

'No. You go back, Mickey. I'll do it alone.'

One reason I wanted him to go back was because if I found what I dreaded to find, I'd want to be alone with my grief.

I think he understood because he just pressed my arm and I heard his footsteps as he made his cautious way back.

I was alone.

I groped my way forward, stopping at intervals and shouting and the echoes sounded like devils screaming.

I soon realized that this shaft in the rock was an old gusher, made smooth by thousands of years of water washing away sand and debris and leaving behind the hard granite. The dank walls told me that even now, water from above seeped down and out when the rains came.

In my bones, I knew I was on the right track. But where were they and why didn't they respond when I shouted, for the echoes of my voice boomed round and round that vast place? Surely if they were there they would hear me?

I got the answer to that when I came into a large cavern. They were there, bound and gagged back to back and they were placed on a shoulder-high slab of rock surrounded by mud.

There was a tiny beam of light coming from a chimney in the rock, and I could feel a draft of air. I lit my makeshift torch to take in my surroundings fearful of some trap like an unseen hold or even a mantrap.

There was nothing so I plunged into the mud and clambered up the slippery sides of rock and quickly freed my youngsters. They were in a state of collapse. Tabby was shivering with cold and hunger, her eyes looking too big for her face. Billy was blue with cold. He moved stiffly as if his ribs were giving him hell, but he kept a stiff upper lip and I was proud of him.

I hugged them close. At that moment they were my most precious possessions. I'm not ashamed to say I cried.

Then I pulled myself together. My voice was hoarse. 'How many of them were they?'

'Four with the Mex. He was in charge and stayed behind when the others joined the rest of the gang. The Mex is known as Blade because of his love of the knife. He threatened to cut us up if you didn't let Grainger buy the land.' Billy's voice trailed away. He was struggling not to cry.

I put an arm about him.

'There's only the Mex. We shot the others.' I patted his shoulder. 'Let it all come out, son. There's no shame in crying.' I held Tabby close while Billy struggled with his emotions caused by relief.

I took a swift look about me as I waited for the storm to finish and then when Billy quietened I asked him as the homemade torch fizzled out,

'What is this place, Billy? Where are we?'

'It's a sacred place known by the Indians. The Mex said that during the rains that chimney turned into a waterfall and the Spirit of the Water came and there was great healing and the Indians came and worshipped and they danced in the cavern and there was an oracle, an old hermit who looked after the sacred place but who has been dead for many years.'

'How did he know all this and where is he now?'

'He said his grandmother was a Kyowa-Apache brought as a prisoner to these parts. As to where Blade is now, I don't know. He comes and goes.'

'Has he fed you?'

'Yes, twice. Tortillas and water. Grainger wanted us alive or I think Blade would have killed us both.'

'Do you think you can manage to walk the tunnel so we can get out?'

He nodded.

'I think if you look behind that rock over there, you might find a lantern. The Mex had a storehouse of stuff.'

I left Tabby clinging to Billy and felt my way to the rock, my makeshift torch flickering and dying. Sure enough I found the lantern and some lucifers and what was more important, some stale tortillas and a coffeepot with coffee-grounds still inside.

I took what I could carry and returned.

'Now you're sure there's no other way out?'

Billy shook his head.

'Blade said that farther up is the sacred spring of the water spirit which wells up and overflows when the rains come. He laughed and said if the rains came before we were freed, we should be drowned. Everything is swept away when the floods begin.'

'The bastard! So we must return the way we came?'

'Yes, he came and went through the tunnel. We came that way and unless there is a side opening I know nothing about he must come in that way.'

'So if he was to come now, then Mickey would come upon him?'

Suddenly I was uneasy. Mickey wouldn't be expecting trouble. 'Come on, let's go.' I swept Tabby up into my arms after lighting the lantern and I strode ahead, Tabby's light frame being no hindrance.

But I had to slow down when I heard Billy gasp and groan behind me. He was being left behind. I put Tabby down and settled her with her back to the rock.

'Don't be frightened, sweetheart. I'll be back,' and I left her the lantern and groped my way back to Billy. I hooked his arm about my neck but when I came to move him, he collapsed.

'It's no good, Pa, it's my ribs. He kicked my bad side. You'll have to go on without me and I'll follow as best I can.'

I felt his side and there was the telltale swelling and Billy cringed. I felt him tremble and hold his breath. A rage, greater than I'd ever experienced before enveloped me. Nobody, but nobody was going to treat my family the way he had and get away with it!

It was then I heard Tabby scream and keep on screaming. My rage turned to fear. I ran back along the passage but there was no light and no Tabby. The screams had stopped abruptly.

I dropped to my knees, and beat my head against the ground, shock and fear and anger sending me crazy ....

EIGHT

I knelt long enough to control my seething brain and gradually my wits returned. I would have to get Billy out of that place and then get on the track of that bastard. I was charging my way regardless of unseen obstacles back to Billy, thanking God that most of the way was smooth because of flood water.

I found him moving at a snail's pace, feeling his way along the rock wall.

'Billy, he's got her. God knows what's happened to Mickey. We've got to get a move-on. I'm going to carry you and it's going to hurt. Understand?'

'Yes.' The word was a groan but I hardened my heart. This wasn't a time for consideration. I lifted him as gently as I could but nevertheless I knew it was agony for him.

He was a big lad and he wasn't so easy to carry as Tabby was. Each step was agony for him. I closed my mind to his gasps and strode on, fear in my heart for my daughter.

We found Mickey in a welter of blood, not far from the entrance. His throat was cut. I was nearly all in myself and the sight of Mickey threw me. He'd been a good foreman but also he'd been a friend.

'Billy, I'm going to rustle up a fire and make you some coffee and I'll leave the food and then I'm going to go find the horses if they're still around. You've got to stay here and I'll get someone to come for you. I promise.'

Billy looked at me all grave like.

'But what if ...?'

I stopped him. 'Don't think that way, son. I'm going after that Mex and I'll find him. I'll follow his trail to hell! But before I do, I'll sure run into one of the hands out looking for you. You'll make it home, son. I know it.'

I put a comforting hand on his shoulder and his hand covered mine.

'I'll be fine, Pa. Why, with coffee and grub in me, I'll most likely be able to ride, that is, if the horses are where you tethered 'em.'

They were and I led both horses back to where Billy lay against a rock. We both felt better after some strong but smoky coffee drunk rough from the coffeepot. I stuffed down one of the tortillas and left the rest with Billy.

I looked back as I rode away and raised a hand. Billy did likewise. He also managed a lop-sided grin. I was proud of him. As a youngster, he was one of the best.

The first thing I did was to cast around, Indian-fashion and pick up the Mex's trail. He was riding double and the horse's prints went deep. It wasn't hard to find when you knew what you were looking for.

The greaser was riding in a straight line due south and I wondered where he was headed. It looked very much like he was headed for the far mountains. If so, it meant a long hard ride and his horse could falter. On the other hand he could double back and disappear into our own local canyons.

It was going to be a gruelling ride.

I wondered if the Mex knew about Tad Grainger's demise and what would be his plans now. Kidnap, ransom, or just plain bad-minded revenge. If it was revenge, then anything could happen to Tabby from rape to slavery. I knew that white virgins made big money down in Mexico. At least if that was his intention he would leave her alone.

I took heart. I concentrated on catching him rather than weakening myself with crazy ideas of what might happen to her. At the rate he was travelling there would be no chance of him violating her at present.

I steadied the mare to a pace she could keep up for hours and it also gave me the opportunity to watch the trail. A flurry of sand, an overturned stone, a scrape of a horse's belly through scrub told me I was still on the right track.

He was travelling fast, too fast for the horse he was riding. I doubted it was used to carrying the extra weight. It was going to be a matter of waiting for the horse to falter ....

Suddenly in the distance was the sound that all cowpunchers dread, the rolling thunder of many hooves and the sound coming louder by the minute. Far to the west was a gigantic dust-cloud glooming the sky and I calculated that it was coming from down the valley and I guessed some of those dirt-farmers had caused the stampede by rounding up stray cattle and sending them on the run.

It couldn't have happened at a worse time.

I watched the skyline and got a spine-chilling tingle as I saw the leaders come into view. My horse too reacted by lengthening her stride and going at a mad gallop that I didn't try to control. Her speed was going to save my life.

And it did.

We were nearly clear as the maddened steers, heads down, charged across the plain. The mare was experienced with cattle and as we got mixed in with some of the slower cows running with calves, the mare instinctively turned and ran with them. The noise was ear-splitting, calves bawling and cows jostling each other and the overall pounding of hooves like sounds from hell.

Gradually we filtered out of the flow and spying a piece of raised ground and a jumble of rocks I yanked on the reins and we were between two huge boulders, the mare's ribs heaving and her nostrils flaring. I was covered in her sweat foam and I'd lost my hat along the way. My legs were bruised from coming in contact with charging beasts, but I considered myself lucky to be alive.

I stepped down and using my bandana rubbed the mare down and then examined her legs and fetlocks and finally her hooves for damage. She trembled and her bellows still blew but she was unharmed. I breathed a sigh of relief for a man was nothing without his horse.

The stragglers passed by but I gave the mare time to recuperate. I needed time myself. My body ached and I was made aware that I wasn't a youth anymore. I was heartsick too, which turns a man weak. I was at my lowest I'd ever been in my life.

The shadows were lengthening when I finally found strength to start hunting again for that telltale trail. It was well and truly obliterated. It couldn't have been better for the Mex than if he'd planned the stampede himself.

I cursed but carried on and it was while painstakingly looking for sign that I met the old prospector holed up with his donkey for the night. He gave me hot coffee and a plate of badly cooked beans which later would bring on a farting spell, but I didn't care. They filled my belly.

He also gave me news of a rider who was carrying a female in front of him. He was riding south-west. I thanked him and gave him a dollar after he promised to go and seek help for Billy. He knew all about the Indians' sacred ground. I rode away, a little lighter in my mind.

We were heading for the bleak Thunder Mountains, a range of hills that only the Indians in the old days roamed. I myself had never tackled them. There was no grass, no brush and only a few stunted trees and the wind blew all the time down from the north. At some time, miners had explored it and as I rode I passed many ancient mineheads with rusting tools and crude buildings decaying away.

It must have been the place God forgot and yet the tracks led on. I followed.

Gradually the way became rough and more boulders appeared and the tracks meandered around high needles of rock and I became cautious as it became clear I was riding into one of those long deep canyons as the sides came higher and closer. It was like as if the earth had been slashed open.

At least now there was water trickling from a stream and at its edges, a fuzz of green, not much but enough to keep an animal alive. I let the mare drink and crop the grass while I took a look-see. I was beginning to get a definite tingle in the middle of my back and I didn't like it.

I ground-hobbled the mare. I knew she wouldn't stray far from the fodder. I could climb the rocks and go where she couldn't. I took my rifle from its boot and made sure it was loaded. I also took extra shells for it and my Colts. I was a walking arsenal.

If that bastard was holed up, I was going to be ready for him.

I followed the horse tracks, but now they were lighter so I watched out for his footprints. He was a devious sonofabitch. There must be some Indian in him, I guessed but I was mighty puzzled as to why he should catwalk up this lonely canyon. The trail took me back along the stream aways but the going got tough as scrub bushes and mesquite strove with each other to survive near the small stream.

I waded into the trickle of water which ran over stones and made slow going but it was better than being torn by mesquite thorns. It was that thought that made me think about the Mex and Tabby and I could have kicked myself. They hadn't thrust their way through the thickets! I'd been following a bloody horse!

I looked around me and saw nothing but stunted trees and on both sides of me the rearing walls of the canyon which were now like vicious cuts in the very earth itself.

I could see no caves, no signs of life only an occasional bird that sailed silently in the air, watchful for anything that moved. I took store by birds and watched the two circling around for any sign of disturbance and concluded that wherever the Mex was headed, he'd got there and was now snug.

I retraced my steps until I came to the place I'd stepped into the water. I cast around back-tracking. There had to be a place where Blade with Tabby had left the animal.

Then I neared the place where the animal had danced about and suddenly taken off and it was as if I could see the Mex slap the horse's rump and the startled beast jump forward and run.

I cursed myself not for noticing that before, but of course now I was looking for something special. Then, I wasn't.

So carefully and quietly I moved around, crouched low and brought every Indian trick I knew into play. I slid through the brush so that nothing stirred. I put each foot forward carefully so as not to disturb a dry stick or frighten a bird or animal.

It was a long slow job but patience was one of

the best qualities, my old pa used to say.

But patience and skill weren't enough that day. I must say now by hindsight that I blundered. The greaser was more skilled than I'd expected. He'd had the time to stash Tabby and was on his way back to watch out for trouble.

The first I heard that he was near was when the click of his gun behind me froze me solid.

'You're smart, Drexel. I didn't figure you'd get on my trail so soon. You're a half a day in front of yourself.'

A wave of fury erupted in me which was hard to control. Here was the son of a hell bitch and I couldn't do anything about it! I half turned but he stopped me.

'Don't move, Drexel. I want to see both hands. You can drop that rifle for a start.'

I did so. I knew when not to argue. I waited. Was he taking me to see Tabby?

'My daughter, is she all right?'

'Yes. I haven't touched her if that is what's on your mind.'

'Good. I was expecting a pig to act like a pig!'

I heard him laugh. 'You don't anger me like that, *señor*. Now turn round slowly, hands in the air.' I turned and faced him for the first time.

He was a little runt. He looked like a boy of fourteen, but his movements were quick. Before I knew it, he'd pulled my Colts and waved them under my nose with a grin on his face I should have loved to punch away.

'I think we must talk, *señor*.'

'Go on then, talk.'

I was studying him as I spoke. His size belied his age. There were lines about his eyes that spoke of experiences not known by a boy. His face was a fretwork of lines like a map. I reckoned him to be about thirty years old or older. The youthfulness in him was crumbling. He couldn't even grow a decent moustache. His was straggly and his chin was smooth ....

I reckoned he was one of these pretty boys I'd heard about but never met before. And I was glad of it because he wouldn't touch Tabby in that way.

'Go on then, talk.'

'What will you pay for the girl? She'll fetch a good price in Chihuahua. You know they pay good money down there for a virgin and no questions asked.'

'You devil!' I lunged forward and quick as a flash one of the guns came up and a slug whistled past my ear.

'There's nothing to stop me killing you now, *señor*, but I should rather take money from you than risk the girl dying on the long journey to Chihuahua, besides the risk of her being raped on the way. I could be tempted by a good price, *señor*, and she would still be very saleable even if she wasn't a virgin when we finally got there. She could be tired and worn, but she would still be fresh enough for a would-be buyer. Now I know you wouldn't want that to happen, *señor*. Just how high do you value your daughter, *señor*?'

'I should want to see her first, mister. How do I know she's still alive?'

'You must take my word for it. She's alive all right, and at this moment safe from physical harm. If I kill you and start the long journey south, she'll have to take her chances. You understand me?'

I understood him very well.

'I'll pay three thousand dollars and that's all the cash I have in the bank,' I said abruptly and I saw his eyes gleam. I reckoned if Tabby slept with a dozen men in a day, she wouldn't make that much before she got to Chihuahua and she certainly wouldn't be worth much when she got there.

'How will you get the money?'

'Figure that out for yourself, mister. All I want is to see my girl.'

'If I take you to her will you promise on her life to bring the money?' I nodded, anything to get to my little Tabby. I wasn't figuring on holding to promises or such. I would see which way the cat jumped when I got my girl into my sights.

He was suspicious. I could see he was in a bit of a quandary. Could he trust me? Then he took out his knife from the pouch between his shoulder-blades and ran the keen edge along his thumb. It showed a faint streak of blood. I knew that gesture was a threat. In a low voice he said quietly, 'It would be so easy to slit her throat, *señor*, if you were stupid enough to do the double-cross.'

I nodded. He didn't have to convince me. I knew he was soulless, without conscience. You could see it in the flat, bleak eyes. He would kill his own mother if need be.

'Take me to her.' He reacted to the command in my voice.

He motioned with his knife.

'Move ahead, follow the stream and I'll tell you when to turn off.'

I took a couple of steps, muscles tensing and as he stopped to pick up my rifle as I'd figured, I whipped around and chopped him on the back of the neck. He rode the blow or else I should have snapped his neck clean, but he was off balance and went sprawling. As quick as my brain could react I was on top of him and shaking him like a rat. But he was as agile as an eel and slid through my hands turning and catching me in the stomach. I was gasping but managed to hang on to a foot as he lashed out at me.

Then it turned into a rough-house, kicking and gouging and though he was small he was experienced in barroom brawls. His knife caught my shoulder and bit deep. I managed to get my hands on his neck and put all my strength into the big squeeze. He thrashed about and his eyes bulged until he was in danger of choking.

At that point I thought it was nearly over as he was turning black and I eased my aching hands a little. That was my big mistake. A mighty heave and the sonofabitch was free. He lashed out with his knife and caught my ear, nearly severing it. Hot, sticky blood poured from it and as I dodged back, he, panting and heaving, scrambled away and it took me some seconds to get after him.

I was swamped with blood, and I lurched after him, cursing raggedly at my stupid mistake. I should have had him. Another few minutes and I should have choked the life out of him. But my trouble was that I was not a natural killer.

I followed him as best I could. I followed the sound of him crashing through mesquite and bushes and suddenly the trail left the stream. I had no gun and I didn't know how I should face him but at that time it didn't seem to matter. My whole mind was on getting the bastard within my grasp.

It seemed as if we were working our way towards the cliffs which now showed more clearly. Then, above a huge area of prickly pear which grew to more than a man's height, I saw him climbing a narrow path and I figured there must be a trail through that horrendous growth of cactus.

For a moment in time I watched him as he climbed. He was lithe and sure and I knew he'd climbed this way many times. He was even careless and once turned to wave at me mockingly. Then he reached out with hands and feet and he was climbing like a monkey.

I tore my way through the cactus, huge prickles from the flat succulent appendages tearing at my flesh, and my clothes were fast becoming rags. I scarcely felt the pain. I was too enraged that he had got away from me.

Then as I neared the cliff and easier going, the Mex turned and standing on a ledge, leaned back and levelled my own rifle at me. Two slugs sliced huge chunks out of the prickly pear close by and I was showered with thorns.

But I was oblivious to the damage they were doing, for incredibly I watched the terror contorting the Mex's face as he slipped, the rifle with its peculiar kick-back which I was used to, falling from his hand as he frantically grabbed for any hold he could find.

I watched as he scrabbled at the rock in vain.

I watched as his body started to slide and jerk, legs kicking, hands and arms waving wildly. And I watched as he plunged down into that sea of prickly pear and the thorns invaded his body ....

I listened to his screams for the more he struggled the more entangled he became.

I started to climb the cliff and only looked back once and already his body was like a side of raw beef.

I climbed and followed his fresh trail, praying as I'd never done before. My life and that of my Tabby was in the balance. I couldn't make any mistakes, for her sake.

Gasping I finally reached an opening in the rock. It was an insignificant slit, and a man must turn sideways to enter. It was dry and airy inside and the rock itself showed signs of soot as if at sometime the cave had been used as a dwelling place.

I found Tabby with bound wrists and ankles laid in a crevice in a dim corner. It was instinct that made me explore the walls looking for another opening. There was no opening. It was a natural split between a mighty jumble of rocks which had spilled out during some great earth-shattering movement thousands of years ago. There were many such places in this region.

I knelt beside her.

'Tabby, honey, are you all right?'

Her eyes opened slowly. She looked pinched and white and she smelled badly.

'Pa, is that you, or am I dreaming?'

'It's me, sweetheart, come to take you home.'

'And that bad man? Where is he?'

'Don't think about him. He won't trouble you again.' I loosed her bonds and she clung to me and cried.

Tabby looked beautiful in a new blue dress, the day Ruth and I faced the preacher in Wichita. It was the first time Ruth had shed her widow's black and she took my breath away in a pretty lavender dress edged with cream lace. She wore the hat I'd bought and the gloves and carried the parasol. I was real proud.

Her hand had healed although she still complained of a little stiffness when she came to knead dough or grip the butterpats during buttermaking.

Billy was well on the way to recovery and he and Tommy looked unfamiliar in store clothes and a decent haircut.

Tommy had grown and filled out a little and he was the one who'd changed the most. He was thoughtful and still hadn't got over the past ordeals. In some ways he seemed older than Billy.

Me? I started to wear my hair long and over my ears. The good doc sewed my ear back but there was a ragged scar. Doc Carruthers was never good with a needle especially when he was drunk. I was never a good-looking guy anyway, but as Ruth thinks I'm fine the way I am, that's all right by me.

We're now waiting for the train to come in to

Wichita bringing Jesse Coates's sister and her family from Chicago. That in itself is another story. Ruth's brother Joe sent all the details we knew about Jane to a good lawyer in Chicago who soon found her by way of her husband working in the Supreme Meatpacking Company of Chicago. After searching out old documents the lawyer advised her to approach the State Judge and put in a claim for the J Bar C ranch. Now the family were coming to claim Jane's inheritance and start a new life.

Tabby and the boys were excited when they learned there would be two girls and two boys for them to get to know. Me and Ruth and the oldsters were pleased that now there would be no more feuding. It looked as if we might be giving help and advice to the newcomers seeing as they had no experience.

As for poor old Jesse's murder, we had Joe to thank for the final outcome. He kept ferreting around and came up with an old drunk who'd actually seen the shooting but had kept quiet until after he knew that Tad Grainger was dead and couldn't backshoot him himself.

As the old soak told it, Jesse had come from the bank and he'd had a full saddle-bag over his arm and the old man had reckoned he must have the ranch's payroll or some such. Then as he'd walked down the dark alley to the livery stable, one shot had been fired and Jesse had gone sprawling and the old drunk had belly-crawled behind a horse-trough and watched. Then a figure had run softly from down the alley and stopped and picked up the saddle-bag and as he'd run back down to the main street, the light from Pete's saloon had showed up the face of Tad Grainger.

When the circuit judge came to town, old Solly had been sobered up by having a night in jail and being prodded by Joe to tell his story. Young Billy was off the hook and those who'd shunned him and wanted to string him up, now came to shake hands with him. Folks are strange.

Billy very rarely goes into town and our business is done in Wichita. For us, Sweetwater Springs is a no-go area. But Joe, who is still sheriff, visits often and keeps the oldsters supplied with gossip. Incidentally he's sparking Miss Pierce because he misses Ruth's housekeeping.

The boys still thunder into Sweetwater Springs on Saturday nights when they want to stir up some excitement. They only need mention Billy and the near lynching, and fists fly. Sometimes I wish I could bring myself to go with them when I want a bit of raw excitement, but these days I watch myself. I'm responsible for my family and my outfit. If they want to go looking for bruises, so be it, but I need to look after Ruth and my kids and the two old ones.

I must have changed quite a lot. Ruth grins and says I have and I like it. The meanness seems to have melted away. I can even tolerate the Hitchens family and I can think of Amelia without getting stirrings of bitterness.

Mind you, a lot of that is because Ruth and I've been doing a bit of catching up on our love lives. She's happy and nothing like a frustrated widow these days; and for me, well, just say I don't need an Alice Symons, I've got someone even better at home!